"You bought those toys for her?" Angela asked.

"Eric's sister has that boutique in town—Handmade for Baby. Everything guaranteed to be nonallergenic and eco-friendly."

"But so many? There must be ten—"

"Eleven," he interrupted. "Couldn't choose between them, so I bought them all. Figured Sarah would decide which ones she likes, and the rest I'll donate to the hospital." He set Sarah down among the stuffed bunnies and giraffes.

"I think my daughter is going to like all of them."

Mark didn't answer for a moment. Just stood there and stared at Sarah, sitting in the stack of animals, looking wide-eyed at them. "I hope she does," he said, his voice a little gravelly. He cleared his throat, then faced Angela. "A young lady can never have too many stuffed animals, can she?"

"You're a real softy, you know that?" So much so, she was tempted to kiss him.

Dear Reader,

It is such a privilege to be back with this last book of my Mountain Village Hospital series. I've loved being able to develop continuing characters across these stories. I've especially loved writing this last book because it touches on a subject that's near to my heart—juvenile diabetes. *The Baby Who Stole the Doctor's Heart* is a romance in the truest sense—it brings together two people who desperately need second chances at love and unites them as a family. But it also allows Angela, previously a chef at the lodge, to find her true passion. By becoming a hospital dietitian, she creates a situation that teaches children and empowers them to take care of themselves. My hero, Dr. Mark Anderson, is drawn to that strength and conviction in her. He doesn't want to be, but one confrontation with Angela and there's no turning back.

There's no turning back from diabetes, either. But the fight goes on, and one of the great crusaders is Brenda Novak, a fellow Harlequin author. Her son was diagnosed with the disease when he was young, and she's been fighting the battle ever since. Every May, Brenda hosts an online auction from which all proceeds go to diabetes research. Harlequin is one of her biggest supporters. (Thanks, Harlequin!) In 2010 she topped an accumulated $1 million mark! This year, spend a moment checking out her auction on www.BrendaNovak.com, buy an object or make a donation. You can take a peek at my donations, too. As you'll see, I love antique jewelry.

In the meantime, I hope you enjoy *The Baby Who Stole the Doctor's Heart*.

Wishing you health & happiness!

Dianne

THE BABY WHO STOLE
THE DOCTOR'S HEART
Dianne Drake

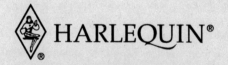

TORONTO • NEW YORK • LONDON
AMSTERDAM • PARIS • SYDNEY • HAMBURG
STOCKHOLM • ATHENS • TOKYO • MILAN • MADRID
PRAGUE • WARSAW • BUDAPEST • AUCKLAND

Recycling programs
for this product may
not exist in your area.

ISBN-13: 978-0-373-06769-5

THE BABY WHO STOLE THE DOCTOR'S HEART

First North American Publication 2011

THE BABY WHO STOLE
THE DOCTOR'S HEART

In this story I've dealt with diabetes—an illness that has touched my life in so many ways. I would like to dedicate this book to Marguerite Holmes, my mother, William White, my uncle, and Keith Kreider, one of the first heroes of my heart—all people I've loved and lost to diabetes. And I would also like to dedicate this book to my friend and fellow author Brenda Novak, whose efforts to raise money for diabetes research will save lives.

CHAPTER ONE

DR. MARK ANDERSON took one more look at the application in his hand, laid it on the desk, facedown, and took off his glasses. "It's not going to be easy, because I like her, but I can't let her into my program. She doesn't fit the criteria, doesn't even come close to the credentials I'm seeing in the other applicants I've looked at."

Drs. Neil Ranard and Eric Ramsey glanced at each other, both of them with expressions on their faces that reflected their support of the decision, mixed with disappointment. "Naturally, we're disappointed, but it's your choice and we support that," Eric said.

"She's your sister-in-law, Eric. And, Neil, she's your wife's best friend. I'm feeling pressured here." Being in White Elk was pressure, staying in medicine was pressure. Everything was pressure these days, and he was already counting down the days until he was done with all of it. Medicine, old life, friends. Everything! Eighteen months to go, and he couldn't wait. But for now he was here, trying to make the best of it because he owed Eric and Neil. They were friends. In better days, best friends. And when they'd asked him to help them start a school to train advanced medical rescue teams, he'd seen it as his chance to pay back all the favors, all the support. After that, though, he was done.

Eric shrugged. "No pressure. Angela's a great dietician.

She has a natural talent for seeing all the connections between health and nutrition. And she's taking on the juvenile diabetes project here at the hospital. But we understand that she doesn't have the kind of medical training you're after. She's eager to learn, but if she doesn't qualify, she doesn't qualify."

"Well, I'm not feeling great about the decision, but I don't want to be saddled with someone who'll hold the program back, and that's what she'll do."

"Saddled?" Neil questioned, arching his eyebrows in surprise. "I wouldn't exactly call being involved with Angela in any way being saddled."

Mark sighed. Angela was a looker, in a cute, pixie sort of way. He did have to admit that. Short, with cropped brown hair, amazing dark brown eyes. And so much sparkle to her. Cute, sexy. Girl-next-door in a most kissable fashion, if he had been inclined to kiss anymore. Which he wasn't. "You know what I mean," he grumbled, shaking her image out of his head.

"Don't envy you the task of rejecting her," Neil said, standing, followed by Eric.

Mark cringed at the thought. "I don't envy myself the task either." He hated rejection. Went out of his way not to be involved in it. But this was one he couldn't help. He didn't have a place for her in his program and he couldn't make a place for her. He had eighteen months to accomplish what should, logically, take two years, and Angela would slow him down. His hands were tied, even though he was the one tying them. "And let me tell you now, this isn't what I bargained for when I came here. I wanted to teach and train, not do the paperwork."

Eric chuckled. "Trust me. Angela is more than paperwork." On that note, the doctors left Mark's office, left him wondering why he'd agreed to this, why he hadn't followed his first impulse and simply walked away.

Truthfully, he didn't know. Didn't want to examine it either, for fear of what he'd find. He'd made his choices, made his decisions, and he wasn't going to change. Sure, he had a detour for the next year and a half, but after that...

Sarah's photo didn't dominate her desk by any means, but Angela's gaze was drawn to it a dozen times an hour. Maybe two dozen times. She'd never known anything or anyone that could fill her heart the way her daughter did. Coming up on Sarah's first birthday, that was all Angela could think about—the last twenty or so tumultuous months, learning she was pregnant, discovering that her husband didn't want a baby or a wife, seeing him flaunt his various affairs on international television. Still, it had been a good time in spite of all that, because of Sarah. "We're doing quite well for ourselves," she said to the photo, then refocused on the meal plan she was devising for Scotty Baxter.

He was seven, with uncontrolled diabetes, and she was worried because he didn't have the home support he needed. His mother rewarded him with snacks, never refused his demands, and most of the time Scotty demanded sweets and foods that weren't good for him. Helen Baxter loved her son the way Angela loved her daughter, but Helen's definition of love was overindulgence, maybe because she was a single mother who was trying to compensate for the lack of a father in Scotty's life. She totally sympathized with Helen, and in some ways she could see that in herself...overindulging Sarah because Sarah's father had walked out. But not overindulgence to the point of harming her, and that's where Scotty and his mother stood right now.

It wasn't a good situation, and she was worried because, so far, she hadn't gotten through. Not to Scotty, not to his mother. She was working on it, though, hoping the camp she was creating—a camp for kids like Scotty—would help. It was coming together, and she was excited by the prospect. One more hurdle, taking the finalized plans to the hospital board, and she'd be set.

Right now, though, she had to concentrate on Scotty's meal plan. "First things first," she said to Sarah's photo, forcing her attention to the computer screen and the list of low glycemic index foods popping up there.

A knock on the door startled her.

"Can I come in?" Mark asked, as he pushed the door open a crack.

Suddenly, she was on tenterhooks. She'd applied to his program. Wanted desperately to be part of the White Elk Mountain Rescue Team, like her sister was. Like all her friends were. She wanted to prove...well, her worth, for one thing. "Sure," she said, saving Scotty's file.

Mark Anderson. Larger than life, filling every inch of her door frame and handsome in a way that defied description. Definitely a man who could make her heart go pitter-patter, if she had a mind to let it. Which she didn't, even though her divorce wasn't stinging so much these days. Truthfully, she didn't have men on her mind, didn't date, didn't want to. Not now. This part of her life was about improvement, about doing the things she'd been deprived of all those years with Brad. About making sure she was in a place where *she* controlled her destiny. It was also about Sarah...Sarah, who always brought a smile to her face. Her life was a good place now, and although she wasn't very far into it yet, she surely did like her direction.

So, no rocking it with someone like Dr. Mark Anderson, even though another time, another place... Fantasies like that allowed, realties forbidden. Besides, in her limited contact with him since he'd helped her and Sarah from the train that had been trapped in an avalanche he'd seemed so standoffish, maybe even grumpy. She wasn't sure why, wasn't inclined to find out. But he held her future in his hand, so to speak, and she did want this opportunity. It was one of so many things she wanted to do and as he strode toward her desk she couldn't wait for him to start. "What did you decide?" she blurted out, too anxious to wait.

"No," he said, quite bluntly.

"No?" Blinking, it took a moment to digest his words. "Did you say no?"

"That's correct. No."

"Meaning you didn't accept me into your program?"

"Meaning I'm looking for people who have more medical training than you do. I'm sorry, but you don't fit my criteria."

He didn't look sorry. In fact, he looked rather bland on the whole subject. "My being a clinical dietician doesn't count for anything? Or the fact that I'm heading up the juvenile diabetes project at the hospital? Or that I'm probably better on skis than most of the instructors at the lodges here?"

"Those are important, even impressive in their own way, Mrs. Blanchard. I'm not diminishing what you're doing here, not trying to belittle your abilities either, but your qualifications are lacking, and I'm not accepting anyone into my program who doesn't meet a certain basic level of medical training. Which you don't. For what it's worth, I knew how much you wanted this, so I went over your application a couple of times, trying to figure out if there was a way I could deviate from the standards I've set for the other students I'll take on. But I couldn't, because if I made an exception for you, I might have to make it for someone else, and pretty soon the whole program would be…diluted."

"Diluted?" She rose from her desk, leaned over it, palms flat on the surface. "You think I'd dilute your program?"

"OK, so maybe that's not the best choice of words. But I think it conveys my intent. I know the kind of background I want in my students, and you don't have it. I'm sorry, but that's my decision. And, to be honest, with all the new programs you're involved with already, I'm not even sure why you'd want to take on something else. Wouldn't that be spreading yourself too thin?"

She steadied her nerves with a deep breath. *That* was none of his business. He hadn't known Brad, hadn't seen the way Brad had put her down every time she'd tried stepping outside herself and doing something worthwhile. Hadn't been there the day they'd come across a skiing accident, found a man who'd crashed into a tree, who had literally been dying before their eyes. She'd tried to help, but Brad had rubbished her attempts and told her the only thing she was good for was calling the ski patrol. Young and frightened, she'd believed him, but still she'd stayed with the man and tried to keep him conscious and talking while Brad had called for help. Unfortunately the man had died on his way to hospital, and she'd always wondered if she could have done something more.

No, none of that was Mark Anderson's business. Neither was the fact that Sarah changed everything. For Sarah, she had to be better, had to know more. For Sarah, she couldn't have doubts.

So, fighting with this man wasn't the answer. She wanted to be in his class, and cool, calm reasoning was the only way she was going to get there. Gathering her wits, Angela decided to resist the battle. "And you don't think hard work and study will overcome what you say are my deficiencies? Because I'll work harder and study more than anybody else you'll have in your class."

"I'm sure you will. But you'd be the only one who wouldn't know the basics on the first day. Basics like how to take a

patient's vital signs. Or how to assess pupillary reaction or
start an IV. I'd have to waste precious time teaching you
how to take a blood-pressure reading when everybody else
is way past that." He exhaled a sharp breath. "What I want,
Mrs. Blanchard, is to teach advanced field work, and you're
not ready for it. I'm sorry."

OK, so he had her there. He was right. She didn't know
the basics. Not yet. But not knowing didn't mean she couldn't
learn. And learn quickly. "Everybody has to start somewhere,
Dr. Anderson. Even *you* attended classes in medical school
where you knew nothing."

"Classes designed to teach beginners. Which is not what
my class is designed to teach. And like I said, I'm sorry. I
know you're going to do some amazing things with your
diabetes program, and I wish you well in that. And who
knows? I'll be gone in eighteen months. Maybe the person
hired to take over for me will have a different set of criteria
for his or her classes." To his credit, Mark actually struggled
with a sympathetic smile as he turned and walked toward
the door.

But Angela wasn't ready to let him leave. In fact, she beat
him to the door. Flew out from behind her desk and practically threw herself in front of Mark. She wanted this! She
wasn't about to take another rejection quite as easily as she
had her ex-husband's. "So, tell me what I can do to make you
change your mind."

Mark's eyebrows shot up in surprise. "What didn't you
understand about me saying no?"

"Trust me, I understand rejection. But I want this and there
has to be something I can do to get myself into your class.
Take some outside courses somewhere, read some books,
take a test. I'm sure my sister will help me…"

Before he answered, he paused, and actually chuckled. Then looked her square in the eyes. "I admire your

determination, and I only hope the students I do choose will have that same determination in them. But classes start in just over a month, Mrs. Blanchard. What you need to know can't be learned in that time. I'm sorry, but my decision is final. Now, if you'll excuse me..."

He laid his hand on the doorknob, tried turning it. Then stopped, like he was waiting for her next round of arguments. Which came immediately. "Is there anything to stop me from auditing your classes?" she asked.

"Auditing?"

"Sitting in, taking notes, learning what the other students are learning?" It wouldn't get her the certificate she needed, but if the instructor who took over the school eighteen months from now was as difficult as Dr. Anderson, at least she'd be prepared. And if waiting for a year and a half was what it took, that's what she'd do. After all, she had time. Plenty of it. "Would you stop me from doing that?"

"I won't certify you at the end."

"I'm aware of that."

"And I won't allow you to participate, as in raising your hand and asking questions or taking part in discussions. You'll sit in the back of the room and take notes, nothing else."

"I'm aware of that, too."

"You won't be allowed to come along on field exercises. Or train on any of the equipment we use."

"That's fine."

"And you won't get progress reports telling you how well, or badly, you're doing."

"Fine, too." It wasn't the way she wanted it, but if this was the only way in for her, she'd take it.

"Well, then, if you want to waste all that time for what's going to amount to nothing, I won't stop you from auditing the classes."

It wasn't an amazing victory, but it was a victory nonetheless. Or at least a tiny step on the road to her goal. "Thank you," she said, stepping away from the door. "I appreciate you letting me do this."

"I'm not *doing* anything, Mrs. Blanchard. Not a thing."

Maybe not. But at least he wasn't stopping her. That was better than nothing.

"She's so beautiful," Angela said, dropping down into the recliner chair next to the bed. "Almost makes me want to have another baby."

"Anything I should know?" Gabby Ranard asked. She was cradling her newborn, Mary, in her arms, looking as happy as any new mother could look.

"I'm not dating, not going to date. Not even liking men too much right now." She reached over and took the baby from Gabby's arms. "Some men, anyway."

"Sounds harsh."

"Not harsh, practical."

"Any particular man?"

"His name is Mark Anderson, and before you defend him because he's your husband's best friend, next to Eric, let me just say that whatever you're going to say will be falling on deaf ears. He turned me down for his training program this morning, and I don't like him, don't want to like him, don't intend to like him." She said the words with a soft edge so not to disturb Mary, who'd already drifted off to sleep. "Should I go put her in the crib for you?" she asked, standing up before Gabby could even answer.

"If you're going to tell me everything then yes. Let her sleep, because I want to hear what happened."

Angela put her goddaughter down, tucked her in and kissed her on the forehead. Even though Sarah was only a year older than Mary, she already missed the baby experience. Loved every minute of it, didn't want it to ever end. But too soon Sarah would outgrow her baby years, then Angela would be having her baby fixes vicariously...through her sister Dinah when she decided to have a baby, maybe even Gabby again. That's just the way it had to be. She wasn't getting any younger, and by the time she'd gotten herself to a place in life where she wanted her and Sarah to be, she just might be too old to have another baby. It wasn't like thirty-three was too old, but if it took her as long to get to the next point in her life as it had to this one, Sarah would be a teenager. Or married and having babies of her own.

"Now, tell me what happened," Gabby urged, after Angela settled herself back into the chair.

"There's really nothing to tell. Because I do work in the medical field now, I thought he'd accept me." Up until six weeks ago she'd been the executive chef at one of the local ski lodges, but the hours Sarah needed didn't work well with the hours her job had required. More than that, Eric and Neil had been trying to recruit her to the hospital to take over the juvenile diabetes program. It had been a providential move, one that had launched her into a totally new frame of mind about her life, and what she wanted to accomplish. Truly, it was time to make herself useful. Make up for all those worthless years with Brad. "And you know how good I am on skis. I'd hoped that wandering around Europe, from slope to slope, all those years, would make a difference. But it didn't. Dr. Anderson turned me down because I don't have what he wants."

"What does he want?" Gabby asked.

"The sun, the moon and someone who knows how to take blood pressure. I'm a good clinical dietician, but I don't even know one end of a blood-pressure cuff from another."

"Sphygmomanometer," Gabby interrupted.

"What?"

"Sphygmomanometer. Blood-pressure cuff. That's the correct name for it."

"See what I mean? I don't know those things, so that disqualifies me."

"Even after Neil and Eric recommended you?"

"Apparently so."

"I'm sorry," Gabby said. "I haven't been paying much attention to what Neil has been saying about the program. With just having the baby and all."

"Two babies," Angela reminded her.

"Two babies, a year apart. That's kept me preoccupied. But I really thought…"

Angela held out her hand to stop her. "It doesn't matter. Dr. Anderson is probably right, much as I hate to admit it. If my ignorance would hold the class back, I don't want to do that. But I've got a plan."

Gabby laughed. "Why am I not surprised?"

Angela mellowed a bit. Gabrielle Evans Ranard was the best friend she'd ever had, next to Dinah. And Dinah didn't count because she was Angela's sister, and that relationship went without saying. But Gabby…she'd come to town, showed up in White Elk totally lost, much like Angela was feeling right now. Then she'd found everything—her life, her love, her happiness. It was out there, and not so far away, Angela hoped. She had Sarah, and that was the first part. The best part. "You're not surprised because you've seen my list."

"Your *long* list," Gabby corrected.

"OK, so maybe I have a few too many goals. Dr. Anderson even said something to that effect, but I know what it's like not having *any* goals, not having anything to look forward to day in and day out. So a few extra goals are good."

"If you don't get so caught up in achieving goals that you miss something else."

"What would I miss?"

"What is it they say about stopping to smell the roses? Well, sometimes it's nice to stop and smell the aftershave, too."

"You're not talking about…?"

Gabby shrugged. Smiled. Didn't comment.

"Well, for your information, he doesn't wear aftershave. I smelled soap on him, that's all. And the only thing I want to smell is the scent of pine trees when I'm called out on a rescue operation. So, I'm going to audit his class. Sit in the back row so I don't even have to smell soap on him, and learn what I need to know so I can apply to the next class…one *he* won't be teaching."

"You smelled soap on him?" Gabby teased. "How close, exactly, were you?"

Angela shook her head. "Were you listening to *anything* I said?"

"OK, so I got sidetracked. But you're so…so animated. It's the first time since Brad that I've seen you react this way to a man, and it just seemed to me that…"

Angela held out her hand to stop her. "He's grumpy. He keeps to himself. He's not friendly. What, in that description, makes you think I'd have anything to do with him?"

"Well, for what it's worth, he's had a very rough couple of years."

"And you and I haven't? You've had two babies and survived an avalanche. I had one baby, a cheating husband, and I survived that same avalanche. That's all rough, Gabby. But we're not grumpy."

"But I have Neil, as well as Bryce and Mary. You have Sarah. Whatever we went through was worth it to get everything we have. And we do have a lot, Angela. We've both been blessed in so many ways I can't even describe it. But Mark…" She trailed off and shrugged.

"You're right," Angela whispered, thinking about Sarah again. "We do have everything, don't we?"

"Neil and Eric brought him here to White Elk because he lost everything."

"Mark?"

Gabby nodded. "It's really not my place to say anything, except he walked away from something that made what you and I've gone through look like a picnic, and at the end of *his* road there was nothing or no one waiting there for him. So he may be a little grumpy right now, but I suppose if anyone has a right to be…"

"OK, so maybe I won't *hate* him. But that doesn't mean I have to like him, does it?"

"Just consider him a means to your end. Audit his classes, learn everything you can from him because, from what Neil tells me, he's an amazing trauma doctor. Then, at the end of eighteen months, ask him to give you a recommendation to the next class." Gabby grinned. "Who knows? Maybe he'll do it. Maybe you'll even enjoy smelling the soap by then."

About the soap, no. Definitely not. But maybe he would give her the recommendation. Or maybe, after eighteen months, when she'd proved herself to be just as good as anyone else he was training, she'd present his words to him on a silver platter and ask him to eat them. It was certainly a satisfying image, one that made her want to run straight to her sister's shelf of medical reference books and start reading. "I brought you a nice fresh fruit salad. It's down in the kitchen. Want some?" she asked Gabby.

"With strawberries?"

"Lots of strawberries." Angela pushed herself up out of the chair and headed downstairs. On the way to the kitchen, though, she stopped in the den and took a look at all the medical volumes belonging to Gabby and Neil. Dozens and dozens of them, all well past anything she could read and understand. But tucked into a corner was an old paperback medical dictionary. Words...medical words with meanings. That was as good a place to start as any, and she was anxious to ask Gabby if she could borrow it. Her fingers were almost trembling as she pulled the book from the shelf. "This is where we begin it all, Sarah," she whispered, as she tucked it under her arm and continued on to the kitchen. "One word at a time."

With, or without, Mark Anderson's help.

CHAPTER TWO

"STAT, from the Latin *statim*, meaning immediately," Angela said as Mark hurried by her in the corridor.

He stopped, turned round. "Excuse me?"

"I said stat, from the Latin *statim*, meaning—"

"I know what it means," he said. "But what I'm wondering is why *you* feel the need to tell me that you know what it means." She arched her eyebrows at him and what he noticed was that they were perfectly sculpted, a lovely frame for the sparkling eyes beneath them. Eyes he stared at for the span of a full five seconds. When he realized that he was staring so intently, he forced a hard blink that shattered the rising sizzle of the moment. *Crazy thoughts*, he scolded himself. *Crazy and stupid.*

"No particular reason."

The heck there wasn't. She was serious about auditing his class, and if he were a betting man, he'd bet a week's pay that she was memorizing a medical dictionary or something as equally bizarre. "I have a hard time believing that you do anything without a reason, Mrs. Blanchard."

"Call me Angela. You're going to be seeing enough of me over the next few months that I don't think we need the formalities standing between us."

"Then you're really serious about this?" As if he didn't already know. Angela Blanchard exuded determination. One look said it all. She squared her shoulders, held her head high, and plunged right into the middle of whatever she wanted, and he doubted an army could stop her. "You're really going to spend the next year and a half of your life sitting in the back of my class, only to reap no benefit?"

She laughed. "Depends on how you define benefit, doesn't it, *Mark*?"

A chill, caused by the way she'd said his name, shot up his arm. Her pronunciation had been crisp, deliberate...rolling off lips he didn't want to look at but caught himself staring at like he'd stared at her eyes an instant ago. And her voice, with just a hint of huskiness... What was it about her that was drawing him? Certainly, she wasn't his type. He liked them long, slim, blond...she was short, rounded in ways he didn't want to think about, athletic. So, after a year or so without a woman, that's all it could be. His retreat into self-imposed celibacy. He was out of his comfort zone, not that he'd had much of a comfort zone lately, and Angela was...tempting. Any man would admit that, and *that* part of him wasn't in retreat quite as deeply as he'd thought. Although he'd been happier when he'd believed it was.

But he could deal with this like he dealt with everything else these days...with indifference. God knew, he'd practiced that to perfection. "Benefit, in practical terms, is the certificate I'll be issuing that will validate eighteen months of study and hard work, that will enable its recipient to become an advanced member of the mountain rescue team and even coordinate rescues on his or her own. Which is a benefit you won't be reaping."

"Your choice, not mine."

"Ah, we finally agree on something."

"Trust me, we don't agree on this. But that will change."

"As in you'll finally come around to my way of thinking?"

She shook her head. "I spent eight years of my life chasing around Europe after a man who, like you, thought I'd come around to his way of thinking. And, foolish girl that I was, I did after a while. So count on my words when I tell you that the last thing I intend on doing now, or ever again, is coming around to *your*, or anybody else's, way of thinking. It isn't going to happen. For me, now, it's all about *my* way of thinking, and doing what I need to do to make a better life for my daughter." She smiled sweetly, her nose wrinkling as the corners of her lips crinkled up. "And I'm really good at that. Better than I ever thought I could be."

Fire and sass. He liked that. In spite of himself, he liked Angela Blanchard. She wasn't put together like any woman he'd ever known up close and personal, and while he definitely wasn't in the market for anything up close and personal, not for a long time to come, he was surprised to discover that he appreciated the contentiousness in her. It had been a long time since anything, or anyone, had challenged him the way she did, and it felt good. Made him feel...almost alive again. "So you're going to content yourself with spending a year and a half that won't produce the outcome you want? Is that *your* way of thinking, to waste your time that way?"

"I'm going to content myself with learning, which is never a waste of time. Whatever happens after that happens." She thrust a packet of papers into his hand. "In the meantime, read this. I'm working on a hospital-sponsored camp for children with diabetes. It's in the last planning stages, and I'm looking for staff support for when I present the final ideas to Neil and Eric. A word from you, *in favor*, would be appreciated. They're going to listen to my presentation tomorrow afternoon, and if things go well, I've already lined up the means to launch the trial run of the camp in a couple of weeks. Take a few kids out and see what works, and what doesn't. The plan was conditionally approved weeks ago and now everything is in place but the hospital's final consent for the trial run, so I'd appreciate you being there to speak up for what a good idea it is."

He smiled—something he hadn't done much of lately. "And you're assuming that I'll support this program?"

"Read the information. It makes sense because it's all about putting the children in charge of their physical condition and their choices. Teaching them to be smarter about their diabetes than the people around them. So, after you've read the literature, you'll support it." A devious little glint flashed in her eyes, and she added, nearly under her breath, "*If* you're as good a doctor as everybody says you are."

Again, that attitude. There was so much of it contained in such a tiny package. He was almost on the verge of finding it sexy. *Almost.* "I'll read the information if I have time. No promises."

"Fair enough." With that, she walked away. No goodbye, no other arguments, and Mark caught himself watching her practically march her way down the hall, almost disappointed when she turned the corner and disappeared from his view without turning back and challenging him one more time.

"Staring at something interesting?" Eric Ramsey asked, coming towards Mark from the opposite direction.

"Not interesting so much as unusual."

"Well, she's certainly a force to be reckoned with. I married her sister, and they're just alike in that aspect. And once you get hooked—"

"Not hooked," Mark interrupted. "And not going to get hooked."

"Just as well, because Angela's living off the list, and there's not a man on it."

"The list?"

"A list of things she wants to accomplish. When she was a chef, she ran her kitchen with the same precision, which

is why we wanted her here, in charge of our dietary department at the hospital. She lives by her lists, and she doesn't
get sidetracked."

A result of those years she'd followed some loser of a man
through Europe? He could definitely imagine Angela living
by the list, but what he couldn't imagine was the carefree
Angela who'd followed the man she'd loved all over Europe
for years. Admittedly, that was a side of her he found intrigu-
ing, a side he wouldn't mind having a peek at. "We all get
sidetracked," he said, half to himself. "Sooner or later, we
all get sidetracked."

Eric patted him on the shoulder then hurried off to tend
a case of bronchitis in exam three, while Mark grabbed up
the next patient chart in the stack. Stomachache. Damn, he
wanted to be somewhere else other than in exam three, treat-
ing a case of nausea.

"Long day?" It was well after what would be considered
normal working hours as Mark took the seat on the opposite
side of the staff lounge. He chose that spot not because he
didn't want to sit closer to Angela but because he wanted
room to stretch his legs. Also, from this distance, without
his glasses, he couldn't see her eyes as well. Wouldn't be so
distracted.

"I'm used to it. When I worked at the lodge, I had a staff
of a twenty-three in the kitchen, not to mention all my other
employees out front, yet I seemed to be the one working
eighteen hours a day, seven days a week. Until I had Sarah.
Then it changed, at least as far as I was concerned. But not
as far as the lodge was concerned. They still needed those
hours from me, and I had a nice, very competent sous chef
who was more than eager to step up into my position when
I could no longer give them what they wanted, or needed."

"Do you miss it?" he asked, trying hard to keep the

conversation limited to neutral topics. He was too tired to argue with her right now. In his frame of mind, she'd probably win.

"Some. I mean, my duties here are so different from what they were at the lodge. I'm doing a lot of administration work and planning, as well as coordinating individual diet plans and doing consults, which means I'm not going to get to cook as much as I did. And I really love cooking. But my job here is…important. It makes a difference. Besides, I have a friend who'll turn over her restaurant kitchen to me any time I feel the hankering to get back to my basics. Catie Lawrence, from Catie's Overlook. Have you eaten there yet?"

"Catie knows me pretty well already," he replied, pulling a chair up in front of the one in which he was seated then propping his legs up on it. "I'm a regular for breakfast every morning, and a semi-regular for dinner. Nice place." Translated to mean nice place to be alone. He sat at an isolated table, didn't have to see people or be bothered by them. It was a situation that suited him just fine since he wasn't in White Elk to make friends, which seemed to go against the unspoken motto of just about the friendliest place he'd ever been in his life. Everybody here *wanted* to make friends. They radiated sincerity and caring, and he sure as heck didn't want all that mishmash coming near him.

"White Elk is filled with nice places. But what's good at Catie's is that while I'm cooking, she'll look after Sarah for me. In fact, she's set up a little nursery in her office for whenever I stop by, or Gabby Ranard stops by with her babies."

"You've been a single mom for a while?" He already knew the answer to that, but asking seemed like the next logical step in the conversation.

"He left me when he found out I was pregnant. But Sarah and I are doing pretty well without him. It wasn't what I'd planned, but life happens, doesn't it? When the bottom drops out of it, you replace it and start over. Being a single mom works quite nicely for both Sarah and me, and I have a lot of support here in White Elk. So, do you have any children?"

"No," he said too quickly, too gruffly. "One marriage on the rocks, no children." And no desire to talk about it either. Just to let her know, he folded his arms tightly across his chest, leaned his head against the chair back, and shut his eyes. This conversation had already gone much further than he'd intended, bordering on private things he didn't get into with anybody, not even with his best friends, and he wanted to end it before it went any further. So, nothing like some nice, rigid body language to convey the message.

"You're not very subtle, you know," Angela said.

"About what?" he asked, instantly regretting that he had. Because asking would lead to more conversation, which he didn't want. Not with anybody, but especially not with Angela. She made him think too hard, made him come too close to the edge of wishing for something he couldn't let himself have. Or even dream of.

"About what you don't want to talk about. You're the one who brought up the subject, in case you've already forgotten that."

He refused to open his eyes, refused to unfold his arms. "How did I bring up the subject?"

"You asked how long I'd been a single mom. Which led to me asking if you had children. It's a natural flow to the conversation we were having, Mark. If you don't want to talk about it, I'd suggest you don't initiate the topic."

Damn, she was a spitfire! Soon to be a thorn in his side, too, if he wasn't careful. "I was making pleasant conversation. Not trying to bring up any particular thing. Saying the first thing about you that came to mind." Well, that was a whopper of a lie. Over the course of the day too many things about Angela had come to mind. Things that had no business being there in the first place but, apparently, had implanted themselves pretty deeply anyway. "You know, trying to be polite."

"Well, your definition of pleasant conversation and mine sure don't agree, because mine doesn't end with my conversation partner turning all grouchy on me, the way you've done."

She just wasn't going to give up. "That might be the case if I were your conversation partner. But I'm not. I'm just a doctor who came in here to put his feet up and rest for a few minutes. Not to be disturbed."

"But—"

"Not to be disturbed," he interrupted.

"All I was going to say was—"

"Not to be disturbed," he repeated. Eyes still closed. Arms still folded. "Disturb. From the Latin *disturbare*, meaning to break up the quietness or serenity of. In other words, break up the quietness or serenity of...me!"

Rather than taking offense, Angela laughed as she pushed herself off her chair. "Look, Sarah is spending the night with her cousins since I'm getting off way past her bedtime, and I'll be headed down to Catie's Overlook in a while. I'm going to cook for a couple of hours, testing my recipe for Chilean sea bass *puttanesca* with seared fingerling potatoes. Catie's thinking about adding it to her menu. So, if you're not quite so disturbed by then, feel free to come and have dinner with me. My treat. Actually, you'll be eating by yourself, but you will be eating my cooking. Which will probably suit you rather nicely, since you'll be dining *undisturbed*."

"Is that a dinner invitation?" he asked, ready to turn her down.

"As in a date for two people, no. As in, if you're hungry, I'll have food, yes. That's an invitation. And normally after my Chilean sea bass *puttanesca*, no one stays grouchy."

He opened his eyes to respond, to turn her down good and proper, in such a fashion that she'd leave him alone from now on, but she was already gone. Which was just as well. Because he had no intention of more interaction with Angela Blanchard, since interaction seemed to lead to…thoughts.

"Damn," he muttered shutting his eyes, then opening them immediately, when the first image that popped into his mind was… "Damn."

"It's crazy," Angela said, handing the diaper bag to her sister, who was already holding onto Sarah for dear life as the toddler struggled to get loose. Which was being encouraged by the twins, Paige and Pippa, who flanked their mother's side, literally bouncing up and down with excitement. Six years old, and they had more energy than Angela had ever seen in any one spot. "He's barely even nice to me, and what do I do? I invite him to Catie's for dinner."

"You're cooking tonight?" Dinah asked.

"Later, after I get off work from the hospital. Trying out a recipe for her."

"So it's not like you two would be sitting down, having a meal together, would it?"

"The two of us can barely be in the same room together, so I don't think we'd survive a meal sitting at the same table. But, no, we won't be together. In fact, we won't even be in the same part of the restaurant. Which is why this will probably work, if he decides to come. He'll be in the dining room, I'll stay in the kitchen, there'll be walls and doors between us. A beautiful start to what's destined to be a rocky relationship." Laughing, she tossed a bag of Sarah's toys at the twins. "Are you sure you want to do this? I mean, I could take Sarah down to Catie's with me. You know how she loves watching her, and she does have the office set up."

"No, Aunt Angela!" the twins cried in unison.

"They've been waiting all day for this. They want to play dress-up with Sarah. I think they also have big plans to decorate the crib as a castle for a fairy princess. And to be honest, I need some baby time. It's nice just…just holding her. And she's not going to tolerate that for too much longer."

"Are you…?" Angela indicated a swollen belly, so not to say the word *pregnant* where the twins would hear.

"Not yet," Dinah said wistfully. "So I think it's the time. If Eric ever has time to slow down a little. That's one of the reasons he brought Mark here, to take up some of the slack while he and Neil spend more family time."

One of the reasons. Gabby had hinted at something else, too, and she wondered if her sister knew. Now wasn't the time to ask, though. Not while the twins were within earshot and Catie was expecting her any minute. "Well, when you do, you know you can count on me for anything."

"For what?" Paige piped up. "What can my mom count on you for?"

"A nice fruit tart I intend to make tonight."

"Me too," the twins cried together.

"You too," Angela said, then gave each of her nieces kisses and hugs. Her nieces… Dinah was a lucky woman, married to a man like Eric who had two such great little girls. They were a good family and she did envy them their family structure. It's what she'd thought…deluded herself into thinking she'd have with Brad, but that hadn't turnd out to be the case. "Fruit tart for everyone. And now I've really got to run."

She paused long enough to give Sarah a kiss. "I'll be back tomorrow, sweetie," she said. "Aunt Dinah is going to take good care of you and I think your cousins have a lot of plans for the evening." She'd spent nights away from her daughter before, but it was never easy. Not even when it was her own sister taking care of Sarah. One more kiss sufficed, though, before the trickle of tears started, then Angela scooted out the door and hurried to her car.

She was already well into her recipe prep, almost two hours now, and as far as she knew Mark hadn't come into the restaurant. Two more hours of work at the hospital after she'd dropped Sarah off and she hadn't seen him there. Now she'd caught herself craning to have a quick look through the pass-through more than she should have, then being oddly disappointed when she didn't see him. But what did she expect? He didn't like her, and while she wouldn't go quite so far as to say she didn't like him, she did recognize that their relationship was strained. Actually, it wasn't even a relationship. More like a walking, breathing case of antagonism that crept up on them whenever the two of them happened to be in the same place at the same time.

He fascinated her, though. She didn't know why, couldn't explain it, and maybe didn't want to. But, yes, he did fascinate her. Which was why, deep down, she'd hoped he would come tonight. No date intended, of course.

"Who would you be looking for?" Catie asked.

"No one."

"Which is why you've been glancing longingly through the pass-through every five minutes for the past hour and a half."

"I invited someone to taste my sea bass, but I haven't been glancing longingly," she snapped.

Catie laughed. "Must be a man, the way you're all riled up."

"A colleague from the hospital."

"Tall, dark and handsome? Likes two eggs over easy, dry wheat toast, a bowl of fruit and black coffee for breakfast every morning?"

"Every morning?" Angela asked.

"Every morning. No variations on a breakfast theme. Not ever."

"Sounds boring."

"Sounds like you're trying to dodge my question," Catie countered, chuckling. "But that's OK. Everybody's entitled to some privacy."

"There's nothing to be private about. He said he has dinner here quite often, and I offered him my Chilean sea bass *puttanesca* if he happened to stop by tonight. Which he hasn't."

"Actually, he has. He's sitting in the alcove. You can't see it from the pass-through. And he did ask for your sea bass, as a matter of fact."

Angela's pulse sped up a blip. Then she took a deep breath to calm herself down. "I'll have it ready for him in seven minutes."

"You could make that a dinner for two, and join him. I mean, it's almost closing time, there aren't many people left in the dining room, and there's really no reason for you being in the kitchen the rest of the evening, since we'll be starting our closing prep in the next half hour. So, cook your meal for him, then join him."

"I can't," she whispered, feeling the heat rising in her cheeks. And it wasn't a heat coming from the kitchen.

"Why not?"

"We don't get along. Not even a little bit. I think that if I were even in the same room with him while he was eating I'd ruin his digestion."

"Yet he specifically wants your sea bass?" Catie shook her head. "If he thought you'd ruin his digestion, he'd have gone somewhere else for dinner. But he didn't. And I think you're being too hard on yourself."

"I don't have time for…for anything. Especially not for…

well, you know. I've got Sarah, and my life is pretty hectic. Even if I didn't ruin his digestion, I still couldn't…have dinner with him. Bad timing. Other priorities."

"Suit yourself. But in my experience, there's always time, if you want it badly enough. And if you do want it badly enough, surprising things can happen, but only if you give them a chance. Personally, I think Chilean sea bass *puttanesca* for two is a good chance to take."

Angela glanced over to the back door, to the great hulk of a man loitering there. Walt Graham, her new medical advisor in her camp program. He was a newly diagnosed diabetic himself, and under the close eye of Catie and her healthy cooking. Also the surprise of Catie's life. Two widowed people, old friends from way back now with one reason to keep them together. No one had seen it coming, but everybody was happy for them. "Maybe for someone else, but I can't take that chance," Angela said, turning to the stove. Seven minutes to fix the meal, then she was going home. Out the back door, not through the dining room.

"I'll admit, it was the best Chilean sea bass *puttanesca* I've ever had," Mark said. The snow was coming down hard for early March. For White Elk that was good as it extended the ski season. And maybe, just maybe, he'd finally find some time to hit the slopes. He'd been intending to for the three months he'd been here, but so far it hadn't happened.

Angela rose from under the hood of her car, and glared at him. "Glad you liked it," she snapped.

"I suppose my logical question here is, are you having car trouble? Or do you simply enjoy tinkering with your carburetor in a heavy snow in a dark parking lot?"

"I'm not tinkering with my carburetor."

He pulled his penlight from his pocket and shined it down,

underneath the car hood. "That's the carburetor, and it looks to me like you're tinkering with it."

"My car won't start," she admitted.

"And you're a mechanic? That's why you're attempting to fix it?" From the look on her face, he figured he was about to get hit with a snowball, but to put himself in the position of the knight in shining armor coming to the rescue of the damsel in distress simply didn't suit him. Oh, he'd help her. It was the only proper thing to do. But he wanted to make sure it was on the terms of the relationship they'd already established for themselves. Contentious. That was the only safe thing to do when he couldn't keep a safe distance from her.

"No, I'm not a mechanic. And I don't know a carburetor from…from anything else under the hood."

"Then I'd suggest you get out from under the hood, get into the car and give it a crank so I can hear what's going on."

"You're going to help me?"

She actually sounded surprised, which made him feel bad. And guilty. She was a nice woman with a tough life. Maybe he didn't want to get involved in all that, but he certainly didn't want his problems heaped on top of hers. "Look, Angela, I know we're got some differences—"

"Big differences," she interrupted.

In spite of himself, he couldn't help smiling. *This* was the Angela that intrigued him. "Big differences. But I never meant you to get the impression that I was downright mean."

"And rude," she supplied.

He chuckled. "OK, mean and rude. But I'm at a bad place in my life right now, which has nothing to do with you. And I really just want to be left alone. Which is hard to do when—"

"When I keep coming at you?"

"Actually, you do keep coming at me, but that's not it. It's…everything." He gestured to the restaurant, to the Three Sisters mountain peaks shadowed in the distance, to the main street of the village. To the parking light, where in the pinkish haze the snowflakes danced like fairy ballerinas. "It's everything. I don't want to be here. Don't want this kind of life. Not medicine, not anything that I've had. But I've got it for the next year and a half, like it or not, and so far you seem to be the one who's always closest when I feel it all closing in around me."

"So, because of proximity, I get the brunt of your bad mood?"

Mark cringed. She was right about that and it made him feel ashamed. Yet something in the very essence of Angela Blanchard made him want to correct his life, and correct it immediately. Whatever it was about her that stirred that frantic beast in him burrowed to the very heart of what he needed. When she wasn't around, he was able to concentrate on the tasks at hand; when she was, that compulsion to change, to try on a different existence nearly consumed him. "Something like that, and I'm sorry. I read your proposal earlier, and I respect what you're trying to do. It looks like an amazing program and I have every intention of speaking up on your behalf tomorrow, and supporting it in the months I'll be here."

"I hope you'll speak on my behalf with a smile on your face, because with the scowl you're usually wearing, Eric and Neil won't be convinced that you really think it's a good idea."

Yes, she did come straight at him and he was beginning to like that directness. "I don't always scowl, do I?"

"About ninety-nine percent of the time."

"Then tomorrow I promise ninety-eight."

"You resist moving by leaps and bounds, don't you? You prefer baby steps."

"And you always move by leaps and bounds."

"Life is short," she said, pulling her scarf tighter around her neck as a gust of wind hit her. "I know there's that poem that talks about not going gently into the good night, and that's how I want to live my life, because there's so much I want to do, and I won't get it done going gently. I lost eight years I can't get back, and I'm not wasting another minute."

"Which is why you want to be a mountain rescue paramedic," he said, feeling a fragile thread of guilt for not including her in the program. But he wasn't going to. If he had to do this, he was going to give it his best, and that included putting the right people in place. As tough as Angela was, she still didn't fit the criteria and, on that, he couldn't budge. "So I assume this is where you're going to make your pitch again? Right?"

"Wrong. You're not getting rid of me, and I intend on being in your class, not in the back row, though. But I accept your decision. Don't like it, but I'll make it work for me."

Which was one of the reasons he couldn't afford any kind of relationship with her. She was so dynamic, so positive. He truly feared it could rub off on him. Truly feared it could make him change his mind about so many things he'd been etching in stone these past couple of years. "Well, right now we need to figure out if we can make your car work for you."

Angela climbed in, turned the key, elicited only a clicking noise. No grinding, no sputtering, no nothing.

"How long's it been since you've had a new battery?" he called out.

"A month. That was my last repair." She tried it again. Still, nothing happened.

So he checked the battery cables and terminals, jiggled, adjusted and had her try one more time, to no avail. "Well, the good news is it's not the carburetor," he said, pulling out from under the hood. "The bad news is it's either the starter or the starter solenoid. Meaning you need a mechanic."

"I've needed a mechanic almost every other week lately. Or it's the time to buy a new car. I've got to find something more dependable because of Sarah." She pulled her cell phone from her pocket. Started to dial.

"Calling a cab?"

She shook her head. "Calling Eric."

"Let him spend the evening with his family. I'll take you home," Mark offered impulsively.

"Are you sure?"

Again, she acted surprised that he had a little niceness in him. He really did have to work on that…*some*. "You fixed me a good dinner. It's the least I can do."

"Then I accept." She tucked her phone in her pocket, grabbed her purse, her briefcase, and her laptop computer from the back of her car. Mark took the laptop and briefcase, and led her to a large black pickup truck that was so high off the ground she wondered if she could get herself inside it without making a complete fool of herself. "Men and their big trucks," she said, hoisting herself up.

"Practical when you're living in the mountains," he said while he waited for her to settle herself.

He was barely inside when she asked, "But you're not going to live in the mountains, are you? Once you've fulfilled your eighteen months, don't you plan on getting out of here?"

"And if I don't need a truck where I'm going, I'll get something else."

"You don't know where you're going?" That didn't surprise her, as Mark seemed more like a man who was running away from something rather than running to it.

"Not a clue. Don't really care. One road's as good as another, and if it leads me someplace else, I'm perfectly fine with that."

Fastening her seat belt, Angela relaxed back into the leather seat, loving the new aroma of it. It reminded her of Mark. Big, manly, bold. "No one's ever sat in this seat before, have they?" It was a strange question to ask, but she couldn't see Mark involved enough with anyone to allow them in this seat, and she wanted to know. Such a solitary man.

"You're the first, except for the salesman who sat there when I took it out for a test drive."

No women. He didn't date. Again, it didn't surprise her, yet, in a way, it did. Men like Mark Anderson didn't live without women. In other circumstances, she could picture him with a woman hanging on each arm. Under these circumstances, though, all she could picture was him alone. And scowling. "I want seventy-five percent tomorrow rather than ninety-eight."

"What?"

"Your scowl. I want you scowling only seventy-five percent of the time. Being all sullen the way you are is bad for your digestion, and while I certainly wouldn't lecture you on all the things that can go wrong with you physiologically when your gut stays in a constant knot, let me just say that nothing good comes of it. So, if you force yourself to quit frowning for a quarter of your day, and even try and smile a little during that time, you're going to relax your gut and feel much better overall."

"And that's your professional opinion?"

"Yes. But that's also the opinion of someone who spent too much time frowning, whose gut was knotted up just like yours."

"What happened to change that?"

"I became happy. Had Sarah, realized the value of my friends. Discovered what I really wanted in my life wasn't as complicated as I was making it out to be. And, most important, I figured out what I didn't want and put an end to it." All of it the truth. When she'd quit letting Brad be the shadow over her that had always held her back, everything had changed. Mark had the same kind of shadow over him, she could see it looming very close, barely allowing him any room to breathe. It was a pity because underneath the scowl she was catching glimpses of something good, and something so conflicted he didn't even know the good was there anymore.

Heading out of the parking lot and turning left onto the main street through town, Angela glanced up to the silhouette of the Three Sisters—three mountain peaks that towered over the entire valley. According to Indian lore, their magic safeguarded White Elk and all the people within their shadow. But theirs was a good shadow. Mark's was not, and it was so heavy she could almost feel it trying to cloud her outlook. It was not a good place to be. In fact, it gave her cold chills. *Come on, Three Sisters*, she said silently to herself. Maybe, just maybe, they had a little of their magic in reserve for Mark, because he really did need it.

CHAPTER THREE

THE short drive was quiet, and once Angela had given Mark directions to her house, she settled back to stare out the window in lieu of tumbling into any sort of dialogue with him. Especially since he was making no effort to talk about anything. The silence between them was a little unnerving, so was sitting so close to him. She didn't know why, didn't know why the hair on her arms seemed especially tingly, or the little chill bumps parading their way up her spine seemed especially charged. But they did, which was why she chose to fix her attention on the road, and on the brisk snow trying its best to lay down a new blanket.

"What the…!" About three minutes into the drive, Mark jammed on the truck's brakes then threw the truck into reverse before it had even come to a complete stop.

The seat belt snapped tight on Angela. "What's wrong?" she gasped, hurled rudely from a nice, relaxed mellow into an immediate panic. She tried tugging the seat belt loose and found it locked down tight across her chest.

"Not sure," he said, looking over his shoulder as he guided the truck backwards. "Thought I saw…"

No more words were spoken. Mark slammed on the truck brakes, and before she could say another thing he'd unfastened his seat belt, hopped out and was already sprinting toward the sidewalk.

"Mark," she called, trying to maneuver herself out of her own seat belt. She wasn't as swift as he'd been about it, and by the time her feet hit the slippery street, he was already half a block a head of her, on his way down the footpath into the city park. "What are you doing?" she cried when she'd almost caught up to him and saw him drop to his knees.

"Saw somebody," he yelled back.

He'd struggled out of his coat by the time she'd reached his side. That's when she saw… "It's Mr. Whetherby. He's the town librarian, and he has dinner at the lodge every Friday night. Lobster Newburg and…" She checked her words when she realized that Richard Whetherby was lying on the ground, not moving, and she was babbling. Immediately, Angela dropped to her knees alongside Mark. "What's wrong with him?" Imitating Mark's actions, she pulled off her own coat and laid it over the still form in the snow.

"Darned if I know. I just saw him lying here…"

"You saw him from the street?" Mark's fingers were busy assessing the pulse in Richard's neck. She recognized that action.

"It's what I do." No other explanation.

"Tell me what I can do." Already, she was pulling her cell phone from her pocket. "Call for an ambulance?"

"Good first step. Tell them he's hypothermic, pulse thready and slow. Tell them we're going to need something to warm him in the ER, and to get one of the orthopedists in—I think we have a serious fracture."

She made the call, told them exactly what Mark had said and, after she had clicked off, while Mark was making an evaluation of Richard's arms and legs, Angela let her fingers stray to the same pulse point Mark had taken a reading from only moments earlier, hoping to learn, at firsthand, what it felt like. And, there it was, slow and thready, like Mark had said. To compare, she felt the pulse in her own neck and was able to determine what a healthy one was compared to the one barely beating at her fingertips. The difference was astonishing. Frightening. For the first time in her life she truly comprehended that she was feeling the very essence of life, and while her essence was strong, Richard's was slipping away.

It didn't take trained medical experience to know that.

"I think it's his hip," Mark said, standing. "Can't tell for sure, but that would be my guess for a primary injury. Everything else going on is probably a result of that. Look, I'm going to run to the truck for my bag. I'll be back right back." He didn't wait for her reply. He simply turned and ran down the footpath with a stride and strength she couldn't have possibly matched. Which left her there alone. Richard Whetherby's only lifeline for the next minute.

"Richard," she said. "It's Angela. Angela Blanchard. I'm here with Mark Anderson, one of the doctors from the hospital. We're going to take good care of you, get you all bundled up and take you to the hospital in just a couple of minutes."

No response, of course. No movement either. Because of that, Angela wanted to feel Richard's life force again, just to reassure herself. So she laid her fingers back on his pulse point, but couldn't find the faint rhythm she'd felt before. Anxiously, she tried again. Moved her fingers from side to side, up and down a little, yet still couldn't find his pulse. Suddenly, it hit her like that proverbial lightning bolt! "Mark," she screamed, rising up on her knees to position Richard's head back a little. She'd taken a CPR class years ago but hadn't ever practiced it except on a dummy. But now… "Mark!" she screamed again as she forced Richard's stiff jaw open and bent to give him a breath. Actually, she gave him several…couldn't remember how many, but she knew it had to be several. Then she reared up, threw off the coat covering the man's chest, pulled his own coat open, placed one of her hands on top of the other, went to the critical spot in his chest she remembered from her instruction, and started to pump. "One, two, three…" she said aloud, fearing she wasn't pressing hard enough, or that she was pressing too hard. She remembered something about bad positioning and broken ribs and punctured lungs.

"Angela!" Mark said, dropping down beside her.

"I couldn't find a pulse," she gasped, scooting aside while he took over the chest compressions. "So I…" Rather than finishing the sentence, she positioned herself at Richard's head, counting each and every one of Mark's chest compressions. "Is it thirty to two?" she asked.

He nodded. Didn't look at her. And as she counted down the thirty, she got ready for the next two breaths, repositioned Richard's head, drew in her own deep breath, then laid her mouth to his. She and Mark alternately repeated their resuscitation efforts for the next few minutes…minutes that felt like an eternity, neither one of them uttering a word as they concentrated on what had to be done. Then, finally, in the distance, came the wail of a siren. A flash of relief passed between them in the fleeting glance they allowed themselves.

"Where are you?" a voice from the road yelled.

"Twenty yards down the footpath," Angela yelled.

"Angela," Mark said. "Can you hold the flashlight, and keep his head tipped back once I get it into position. We need to get him breathing, and I'm going to insert an endotracheal tube into his throat."

The first paramedic resumed the chest compressions, the second broke out the equipment—the tubes, the oxygen, the heart monitor. At Mark's prompt, he handed the ET tube to Angela, who turned it over in her hands, not sure what it was.

"When I ask for it, hand it to me. Until then, just keep the light steady, and make sure that his head doesn't slip. Normally I don't have to get belly down in the snow to do this, and it's going to be a little tricky."

"I can do this," she whispered, more for her own ears to hear than for Mark's. But he heard anyway.

"I know you can." He gave two good squeezes to the resuscitation bag, which had replaced the mouth-to-mouth efforts. "Oh, and when I get the tube in, hand me a stethoscope."

It was all procedural, very matter-of-fact, which amazed her. Step one, step two, step three…a methodical plan they all knew, but she didn't.

"And once I get the tube in, be ready to hold it while I check to make sure it's in the right place."

Now, that scared her a little, but she nodded, hoping her nervousness didn't make her look like one of those dolls with the bobbling heads.

"Ready?" he asked, squeezing the resuscitation bag one last time. Then signaled for the paramedic to stop the chest compressions momentarily.

It happened in the blink of an eye, but she took in everything. Mark positioned Richard's head, she positioned the flashlight. Mark lowered himself flat in the snow, she took hold of Richard's head and held on for dear life. Then Mark took some kind of instrument from his pocket…she couldn't remember its name, but she'd ask him later…opened Richard's mouth even more, then asked for the tube. Instinctively, she moved closer as she handed it to him and, without fanfare or effort, Mark simply slid that tube into Richard's mouth. Not the esophagus, she told herself. This tube was for breathing, so it went into the trachea.

For the first time she wondered about the anatomy of it, wondered what separated the two as they were in the same area. Wondered how Mark differentiated.

"Stethoscope," Mark said. "And hold the tube for me now. Don't let it move."

Angela was immediately in the snow, not on her belly, but close to it, as Mark rose to his knees to listen. The IV paramedic who manned the equipment, and who was also preparing to start an IV, attached the resuscitation bag to the tube, gave it a couple of good squeezes, and Mark nodded.

"Tape it in place," he told Angela, as the paramedic dropped a roll of white tape down to her.

"Tape it?" she asked.

Chest compressions were starting again. Mark was busy doing something with a syringe. The IV paramedic was attaching a bag of fluids to the tubes coming from Richard's arm. So many things were going on and Angela felt more lost than ever in all the procedures. Even the simple ones, like taping the tube.

"Lasso the tape around the tube then anchor it on both sides of Richard's face," Mark explained with all the patience of a good teacher.

So easily said, yet such a daunting thing to do. *For her.* Still, she taped the tube in place as Mark attached the syringe to a tiny tube sticking out of it.

"Blowing up the cuff," he explained. "The small tube leads to an inflatable cuff on the actual breathing tube—endotracheal tube is what it's called—and when air is inserted into the small tube, it gives the endotracheal tube a tight fit to the tracheal walls so it doesn't slip or let air get in around it." He completed the task, then reattached the resuscitation bag to the tube and fell back into the rhythm of thirty compressions, two breaths.

All of this in mere seconds. Angela was amazed. And exhausted by the time they'd stabilized Richard enough to lift him onto the stretcher.

"Don't you have to shock him or something?" she asked.

She'd seen it on TV. Rush in, get the paddles, shock the heart. But they weren't doing that here.

"We've got good oxygenation established to his brain, and it was done quickly. The purpose of CPR is not so much to revive the patient but to keep them oxygenated long enough to get them proper help. The hospital is two blocks from here... better to try the cardioversion there, in a more controlled environment."

Cardioversion...something else to look up.

As Mark explained all this to Angela, the paramedics whisked Richard to the ambulance. And by the time Mark paused for a breath, and Angela had picked up their discarded coats, the ambulance was pulling away. "That was so fast," she whispered. Ten, maybe fifteen minutes, tops, from the time Mark had first spotted him. It was amazing!

"Thanks to you," he said, taking her coat from her, brushing the snow off it then helping her into it.

"I didn't do anything. I just... Look, do you need to follow them to the hospital?"

"I should. As I started this, I'd like to see it through."

"Then you go on. I want to stay here, see if I can find Fred. And clean up the trash we've created." Bags, boxes, tubes...an amazing amount of supplies and trash left behind for such a fast procedure.

"Fred?"

"Richard's dog. A Yorkshire terrier. He walks him out here at night. Everybody in White Elk knows Fred...he spends his days at the library, under the checkout desk. He has special privileges as a service dog."

"Service dog, like for the disabled."

Angela smiled. "The library board was kind when Richard asked for permission to keep Fred with him. The kids who come to the library love the dog, and participation in the various children's programs has gone up since Fred started collaborating in storytime."

"Then you'd better find Fred, or there's going to be a lot of disappointed children. But how are you going to get home?"

"I'll walk. It's not a big deal. You just go to be with Richard. I need time alone to…to think."

Mark didn't run away, though. "I'll wait in the truck for you."

She shook her head, turned her back on him, then started down the path. "Fred," she called. "Come here, Fred." Only when she heard the running of what she already recognized as Mark's engine did she finally break down. Dropped on a nearby park bench, let out a weary sigh, allowed a few tears of emotional exhaustion to slide down her cheeks. What she'd done here tonight…it was so insignificant. But what she'd seen, and what she'd wanted to do… "I want it," she whispered, as a furry little mongrel poked its head out of a bush. "I really want it, Fred, instead of standing on the sidelines, being useless, like I have most of my life." She held down her hand and wiggled her fingers to coax the dog over, still thinking about how, in the span of moments, Mark had shown her so much. She wanted to reflect on everything that had happened, inscribe it in her mind, so she'd never forget. But try as she may, the only thing inscribed there was…Mark. Distant images, up-close images. He was all she could see.

"We don't usually allow dogs in the hospital," Mark said. Angela stood in the hall, clutching Fred and watching as Mark and his team worked on Richard Whetherby. He was still unconscious, dwarfed among all the machines clicking and clacking around his bed, and all the tubes stuck in him. A monitor overhead traced the rhythm of his heart, a ventilator at his side forced breath into his lungs and measured it into some sort of bellows. It was all a strange, new world to Angela, and while she'd spent a good bit of time in hospitals, especially lately, it was as if this was the first time she'd ever really noticed what went on. And it scared her. Yet it also showed her just how much she didn't know, and how much she wanted to know. "I probably should have gone on home and taken him with me, but I wanted to see…to know how Richard's doing. He's a nice man. I used to come out of the kitchen and have dessert with him when he ate at the lodge."

"So far, he's not doing very well," Mark whispered. "We're having trouble getting him stabilized. He was hypothermic… too cold…"

"I know what that means," she said.

"Not sure how long, but it's causing problems with his vital signs. He's not warming up the way we'd like. Everything's sluggish."

"But isn't the cold actually good? Doesn't it slow things down, sort of keep someone in a state of hibernation?" It sounded dumb, but she was curious.

"It does. The body slows down, requires less oxygen, and the cold helps keep things in a more balanced condition."

"But not Richard?"

"Actually, I think the fact that it's so cold is probably what saved him, but he's got another problem, which is causing complications. What we think happened is that he slipped on the ice, broke his hip…a fairly substantial break that caused some internal bleeding. He was probably lying there for quite a while. Went into shock, got too cold for too long…a lot of contributing factors."

"But he'd probably be dead if it weren't for the cold temperature?"

"Probably. It saved him, yet it's making his situation more complicated. He's alive, though, and that's the good thing."

"So he's going to make it?" she asked, hopefully. Even though she no longer cooked at the lodge, she and Sarah still joined him there most Friday nights for dessert. The routine, as insignificant as it seemed, was part of their lives, like the way so many other seemingly insignificant things were here in White Elk. And none of them were really insignificant at all, not even dessert with a kind old man, as they were the things that made up only a small part of the reason she wanted to raise her daughter here.

"Not sure yet. We'll know more in the next twenty-four hours. And even then he's going to require some pretty drastic surgery. Which means that if Mr. Whetherby doesn't have someone at home to take care of his dog…" he reached out and scratched Fred on the head "…looks like you're it."

"No dogs where I live. It's a rental. That's the rule."

"Look, I've got about thirty more minutes here before we get Mr. Whetherby transferred to Intensive Care. Maybe in that time you can find someone who will take the dog temporarily, then I'll drive you home."

She could have called a cab, could have even walked the mile and a half, although it was getting colder out and the snow was coming down a little harder. But she wanted to ride with Mark, wanted to hear him talk about what had happened tonight, wanted to hear his assessment. Anything to keep her connected to the medical moment. So she agreed to ask around the hospital for a temporary home for Fred, only to be turned down time after time. Allergies, other dogs, not enough time to take care of the pup…in thirty minutes she heard every imaginable excuse. Consequently, when she returned to the emergency department in search of Mark, Fred was still bundled into her arms.

"Richard came round," Mark said, pulling on his winter coat. "We took him off the ventilator because he's breathing on his own now, and the first thing he asked was about Fred. Stupid dog means everything to him. Fred's all he has."

"And I can't keep him," she said, feeling bad. She had so much…her daughter, her sister and family, her friends. Yet Richard Whetherby had…his dog. Even that status was in jeopardy if she couldn't find a place for that dog to stay. "Which means I may have to send him to a shelter, and I suppose they'll take care of him for a while, but…"

"I told him I would," Mark said, almost in passing.

"What?"

"The dog. I'll take care of him."

Now, that surprised her. She truly hadn't expected the man who didn't want human involvement to take in a dog. But still waters ran deep, didn't they? Or, in Mark's case, diverted way off the main course of the river. It pleased her, actually, that he could show a little humanity for something outside his job, and she wondered what other surprises he might be hiding. "He's very friendly," she said. "Likes to be carried."

"He'll walk, if he expects to live with me."

Scowl popping out now, but not the one she normally saw. More like one he was trying to force.

"How did you see Richard lying on the footpath, in the snow? It was dark, and he was a good fifty feet off the road. I didn't see him and I've got good eyesight."

"Training," he said, resisting her offer of handing over the dog. "I've practiced my skills of observation more years than I care to count." That's all he said, then he turned and walked toward the exit, taking about ten steps before he turned back to see if she was following.

She was, but slowly. With each step she was looking around. Practicing her own skills of observation. Looking at the various pieces of equipment sitting along the hall walls. Gazing into the various emergency exam rooms to study whatever she could see there, trying to memorize it so she could look it up when she got home.

He watched her studying the things he took for granted. There was such fascination splashed all over her face…something he remembered in himself years ago. Something so far in the past he'd forgotten that he was once just like Angela was…eager and anxious to learn. Except he didn't have the natural skills she did. He'd seen those skills this evening. Observed the way she'd been put into a dire situation and seen how she'd responded, not only to instruction but to her own instincts.

It was nice when he'd been that enthusiastic. It had felt like the whole world was just waiting to happen, and he envied her that. But for him it was gone. More than that, he didn't want that feeling rekindled, and being around Angela he could almost feel the beginning of the embers. "Are you coming?" he asked, but not impatiently. He wanted her to savor the moment, to linger in the face of her first victory. In the years to come, that would be important for her. She wouldn't forget it.

Neither would he.

"Would you like some hot tea, coffee, hot chocolate? With brandy?" She climbed out of the truck, still clinging to Fred. "And I have a fresh apple pie if you'd care for a piece." It was the polite thing to do. She didn't expect he would accept, as the short ride home from the hospital had been tense. Actually, much more than tense. Brutal. Once the truck door had shut, and the engine had been engaged, the cold silence had slipped down, and in that mile-and-a-half ride, it had turned into a frozen block of ice that chilled to the bone. She'd hoped for some chat, maybe for some feedback of what she'd done…right or wrong. But in the darkness of the truck's cab, even though she couldn't make out the detail of his face, she could certainly make out the hard set of it. No mistaking the intent either. He didn't want to talk, didn't want to be bothered. So apart from reminding him of where she lived, the only noise from inside that truck had come from Fred, who'd settled into the seat between them, his head resting on Mark's thigh, and gone to sleep. And snored. Staccato, burbly little snores cutting into the icy quiet.

Then they were sitting in front of her rental condo, and now she was waiting for him to turn down her invitation so she could put a good, solid door between them. Except he didn't turn it down. At least, not right away. In fact, it almost seemed he was considering her offer. "So, what will it be? Apple pie? Coffee only?" Like she needed to ask again. It would only make him turning it down seem even bigger. Poor Angela, couldn't entice him no matter how hard she tried.

"Apple pie is good," he conceded, "if management doesn't mind Fred coming in for a little while."

"I'm allowed guests," she said, very cautiously. Still wondering if he'd really accepted. Because her stomach just flip-flopped. "As long as you hide him in your coat when you bring him in. My next-door neighbor complains if the wind blows in the wrong direction, and she's probably watching us right now."

"She doesn't complain about Sarah?"

"Oh, she does. But the owner has grandchildren, and he loves Sarah. So he doesn't listen to those complaints. But he doesn't want anything in his condo that will chew up carpet or claw the upholstery. I'm allowed a goldfish, that's all."

"Then Fred goes in the coat." With that, he tucked the pint-sized Yorkie under his coat and stepped out of the truck.

Angela was still stunned. She wanted to ask him why he was accepting her invitation then contented herself with the excuse that a late-night snack must have sounded good to him, that maybe the adrenalin flow from the rescue had given him an appetite. What else could it be?

"Most of the furniture isn't mine," she said as they stepped in and Mark put Fred down on the floor to sniff around. "Brad and I lived in a suite at the lodge. We spent our entire marriage living in one lodge suite or another, and when you do that, you don't accumulate many things. Clothes and necessities, that's all."

"It's nice," Mark said, looking around. "Small, basic. More than I need."

"Where do you live? I don't think I know."

"I was going to stay in one of the rooms up at the lodge on the Little Sister, but after it caught on fire...well, I'm renting a room with Laura Spencer now."

"One of her guest cottages, or in her inn?"

"Over the garage to her house. It was a storage room, had plumbing, a bathroom, a place to plug in a microwave. So she shoved all her stored goods down to one end and I'm down at the other. It works."

"Because you're temporary, right?" Angela pulled the pie from her refrigerator—a pie she'd baked that morning, not for any particular reason other than she'd been in the mood to try a new diabetic apple-pie recipe she'd found. "Here eighteen months, then gone. No need for a real place to live. Any storage closet will do."

"Eighteen *long* months. You need to use the qualifier when you mention it because that's the only thing that gives me any hope."

"Any hope?" She glanced over at him as she pulled two plates from the cabinet and grabbed a knife. He was smiling. Simply smiling. "You know, it's hard to tell when you're joking or being serious," she said.

"Just count on me always being serious, and it won't let you down."

"Do you frown at home, too? You know, practice in front of the mirror? Get up and put that frown on first thing in the morning? Frown your way through your coffee and hold onto it afterwards when most morning frowners normally relinquish theirs? Because you seem to have raised it to such an art form. Care for coffee with your pie?"

"What I'd care for is a place to walk Fred. He's a little… hyper. And, yes, I do frown first thing in the morning, as a matter of fact. All the way though my coffee and beyond that."

She glanced over. He was smiling again. One of the nicest smiles she'd ever seen, actually. Too bad he didn't do more of it. "Take him out the sliding glass door. The patio is fenced in. He'll be fine for a few minutes, so long as he doesn't bark."

As she sliced through the pie, then arranged it on plates, she wondered what could make a man who was such a good doctor, and someone who was so observant he knew when a pup had to go out, so distanced from life in general. Divorce could do that, she supposed. That might have been her, actually, if half the population of White Elk hadn't swooped in to take care of her after Brad had gone his merry way. And if she didn't have Sarah. Sarah was the real lifesaver. Sarah… she already missed her.

On impulse, Angela rang her sister to check in. "I know it's kind of late but—"

"I heard you had quite a little adventure tonight," Dinah interrupted.

"It was Mark's adventure. I just stood off to the side and did what I was told."

"Not according to what Mark told Eric. He said you were really good…very quick for someone who's not trained. He told Eric you get as much credit for saving Richard's life as he does."

"He really said that?"

"Eric wouldn't lie."

No, he wouldn't. And while Angela was flattered, she wondered why Mark couldn't have said those things to her himself. "How's Sarah?"

"Probably exhausted. My daughters kept her busy practically every minute she's been here. And when I put her down, she went right to sleep."

"I'll be by in the morning, before work." Thank heavens for the hospital child-care center. It was a blessing for all the parents who worked at the hospital.

"You sound funny, Angela. Are you OK?"

"Just getting ready to warm a couple of pieces of apple pie."

"Two pieces? Who's there with you, if a nosy sister can ask?"

"Sure, she can. Mark's here with me. Outside walking Richard's dog right now. When he brought me home, I asked, didn't expect him to accept, but even the most reclusive of men have to eat, I suppose."

Dinah laughed. "It's about time you start getting out."

"I'm *not* getting out. I'm fixing apple pie, à la mode if he likes ice cream. Then he'll go home, and I'll go to bed, and in the morning we'll barely speak when we bump into each other in the hospital. That's all it is." She glanced over, saw him standing in the patio door, Fred under his arm. "Look, kiss Sarah for me and tell her I love her. And as for you, get it out of your mind."

"You're right. We'll barely speak," Mark said from behind her, putting Fred down a minute later.

She popped the plates of pie into the microwave, then turned around and stared at him, hand on her hip. "And why's that?" she asked, frowning.

"First of all, let me just point out that you're frowning.

Second, no particular reason. It just seems to work out better for me that way." The seat he chose was a hard wooden one at the tiny kitchen table…a table for two. He didn't take his coat off, didn't relax. Simply sat, folded his hands on the table, and went into his silent mode.

"You know you're not very good company, don't you?" Angela finally said, taking care not to frown again.

"You wanted good company? I didn't hear that mentioned in the invitation."

She gave him a long, hard look to see if there was any hint of amusement there. And she did see it once again. It was subtle, but there was a little glint in his eye, if she caught it from the right angle. "If I'd wanted *good* company, I'd have left you in the truck and only invited Fred in."

The corners of his mouth turned up, but barely noticeably. "You begged," he said.

"Excuse me?"

"You begged. The offer of coffee was polite. The pie… definitely begging. Down on your knees for sure, if not for the snow."

"Wishful thinking, *Doctor*. Because I was still at the polite stage. Had I been begging, you'd be getting more than apple pie. I'd be serving it a la mode, and tonight you're *not* getting a la mode." She emphasized that by putting the carton of ice cream she'd pulled from the freezer to soften back into the freezer. "And just so you'll know, the pie is a leftover. And leftovers signify being polite. That's all." Good words, but her heart was racing a mile a minute. More than that, she could feel a flush rising in her cheeks. Whatever he was doing to her wasn't anything any man had ever done before and she was scared to death it would show. So she sidled up to the refrigerator, hoping it would cast some kind of shadow over her. If not, she'd have to crawl in.

"So, do you cook like this for yourself all the time? Pies, sea bass *puttanesca*?"

"Sometimes. Not always. It's a release…an outlet. Helps calm me down when I'm upset or frustrated. Gives me time to think."

"You've been frustrated or upset lately? Is that what begot the pie?"

"A little. And before you ask, yes, you're the cause of it. I'd counted on getting into your class. And your rejection has actually brought about a lot of cooking—new recipes for diabetics I hope to introduce at the hospital." The flush was subsiding now that she was reminded of how he'd turned her down. Then, of all things, praised the abilities that weren't good enough.

He eyed her objectively, the crinkle of a smile returning to his lips. "You pack it in well."

"I don't eat it all. I give it away…friends and family." She removed the pie from the microwave. "And, occasionally, grumpy men who rescue dogs."

"I suppose Dinah told you what I said to Eric, didn't she? Sometimes I forget what a clannish place this is, that everybody is connected to each other in one way or another."

"She told me," Angela said stiffly, as she set the plate in front of Mark, practically threw a fork at him, then choose *not* to sit across from him. It would be too uncomfortable. She didn't want to look at him, didn't want any kind of personal involvement. Which was what compelled her to pull a high stool over to the kitchen counter. "And it would have been nice hearing it from you."

"I compliment you, then what? You think you're going to get a spot in my class? One thing leads to another, we save a life together and naturally you're the most likely candidate to sit front and center, rightfully? Is that what would have happened?"

"Maybe. At least a few days ago. But after tonight…" She shrugged. "It doesn't matter. Just eat your pie before it gets cold, then you and Fred can be on your way and you won't have to worry that something you say might be misconstrued by the dietician." Admittedly, she was a little hurt. Hearing the words from Mark would have meant…something. She wasn't sure what. And now she'd never know.

"So that's why you're sitting halfway across the room? Because I didn't praise you to your face?"

"I'm sitting across the room from you because I choose to, just like you chose not to say anything to me about my performance tonight. I know I wasn't very good. I'm well aware of how little knowledge I have and how, in practical terms, I really wasn't much use to you. But sometimes a pat on the back and the words *good job* go a long way." She cut off a bite of pie, nibbled at it, and suddenly didn't feel like eating. Not alone. Not with Mark either. In fact, all she wanted was to settle in and listen to the gentle breathing of her daughter. That always made everything better. But she didn't even have that tonight, and all of a sudden her tiny condo felt cavernous. And empty. Even with Mark there. "Look, I'm really tired. It just hit me."

"Probably the adrenalin wearing off."

"Probably… Anyway, I'm going to bed. Stay here as long as you like. Eat your pie. Finish mine if you're really hungry. In fact, take what's left home with you." She pushed herself off the stool and didn't even loiter in the kitchen. All she wanted was that door between the two of them, like she'd wanted earlier. If it took her being a bad hostess leaving her guest sitting alone in the kitchen, eating, so be it. She didn't want to be anywhere near Mark Anderson tonight, not even for a few minutes. "So, if you'll excuse me…"

Mark shook his head, and a broad grin broke out all over his face. It showed in his eyes, and in the lines at the corner of his eyes. Showed in laugh lines at the corners of his mouth. Very attractive, she noted, then immediately tried recanting that thought. But it was already too late. In her mind, Mark Anderson had just become framed as attractive. Not brooding, not scowling. Attractive.

"I know I'm a lousy date. Lousy company. Lousy companion. But I'll swear I've never had a woman just get up and leave me eating at the table the way you're about to do."

"In a public restaurant, I might have excused myself to the restroom and run out the back door."

"So you make a habit of this?"

"Honestly, I don't know. The last time I had a man eating at my table...other than my husband... Let's see. It must have been nine years ago, right after I met Brad. We weren't married yet so technically he wasn't my husband. I cooked for him and..." And they'd left the dinner table in the middle of the meal. But they'd left it together and had gone only as far as the bedroom. That thought made her blush. Which was another reason she needed to get away from Mark. Because a brief flash of the two of them heading off to the bedroom crossed her mind. "Anyway, that was a long time ago, and right now I'm tired. So..."

As she slipped past him, he stood, nearly blocking the doorway. Then he patted her on the back. "Job well done," he said. Then he sat right back down and picked up his fork, giving her a little salute with it, before she could react.

Later, in her bedroom, long after she'd heard her front door shut, she was still awake, too wired to sleep. So maybe his little effort there had been conciliatory. She'd coerced him into it. Or he was simply being condescending. Whatever it was, it didn't matter because it *had* been a job well done. She knew that, and felt pleased by it. More importantly, *he* knew that, too. It was on that thought she finally drifted off, dreaming not of Mark so much as working shoulder to shoulder with him. Another time, another emergency, and in her dream *she* was calling the shots.

It was a very pleasant dream indeed.

CHAPTER FOUR

"It's easy for a child to be persuaded, by an adult, to do the wrong thing, and if that adult doesn't know the facts, or disregards them, that child is in jeopardy. You're supposed to trust the adults in your life, and while they might mean well, when your kindly grandfather tells you it's OK to have that little piece of cake, that it will be their secret, it needs to be the child who takes the upper hand and educates the grandfather. And I'm not saying that all adults will sneak cake to diabetic children. Because they won't. But the honest truth is, it's easy to just give in. You know, the notion that one little slipup won't hurt them. But it can. A lifetime of slipups and bad notions will kill them, so they have to learn young to do better, know more, and take control."

Seated at the mahogany conference table for twelve, with everybody else at one end and Angela all by herself at the other—her choice, not theirs—Angela drew in a deep breath, then slumped down a little in the chair. It wasn't a formal hearing. She was among friends. Eric and Neil. Dinah. Walt Graham. Doctors Jane McGinnis and Kent Stafford. James and Fallon Galbraith. And, surprisingly, Mark Anderson. They were facing her; she was facing them, presenting her program.

"I know you've been going forward with it, getting it set

up," Eric said. "But to what extent? How soon can we give it a try?"

"Actually, the lodge up on Little Sister is undergoing major renovation after the fire several months ago. They've redone the secondary kitchen already and they're working on some of the rooms, so it hasn't reopened to the public yet. But they've agreed to let us come and camp out in the part of the lodge that's complete. It's probably not what comes to mind as a traditional camp setting as it's going to be inside, but the lodge management is happy to open up one of the wings for us, and allow me access to a kitchen because they really want to see this camp initiated."

"So you're already lining up candidates?" Neil asked. "I didn't know you'd gotten that far, but I'm impressed."

"I have a list started. In fact, a waiting list because I've already filled up the spots in our first camp session. And I've got to tell you, the people here in White Elk are really excited. When it comes to anything about taking care of their children they're exceptionally supportive." She glanced at Mark, who seemed to be fixed on something far, far away. Saw something in his eyes…sadness? "The town charity Christmas trees were sponsored for it this year." Christmas trees lining the streets of White Elk, donated by the town merchants. Families, companies, individuals paid to decorate the trees, in principle sponsoring them. "And proceeds went to the program here for diabetic children. Half *that* money was set aside for the camp. Also, the parents of the kids who might come…they know this is our launch, that I haven't done anything like this before, and we intend to use this first session as trial and error to see what we need in order to go forward with a regular program. Maybe offer these camps five or six times a year after we work out the details. More often, if we see there's a need for an ongoing program of this type."

"Well, camping in a lodge sounds pretty good to me," Neil said. "Especially as we still have snow on the ground."

"It will vary by the season. One of my goals is to make the camp different every time we offer it. For example, in the winter, we're going to teach the children winter physical fitness as part of the program…skiing, skating. And in the summer concentrate on activities like tennis and swimming. Anything to keep them physically active. I think refresher courses will be good, let them come back whenever they want to, or whenever they feel they need the support. Keep it an open program for these children so they'll always feel like there's somebody there who cares. Hopefully, it will be so fun for them they'll just want to come back for no other reason than being there with kids going through the same thing"

They were with her on this. She could feel it in the way her nerves tingled. See it in the way their eyes stayed glued to her. All except Mark's eyes—his were still staring at something out the window. She glanced, reflexively, to see what he was looking at, and realized it was only the asphalt parking lot. So what was it, somewhere far beyond that parking lot, that was holding onto him? "Also, did I mention that I have contributors?"

Gabby laughed. "About a dozen times."

"Nerves," Angela confessed. "I've been planning what I was going to tell you for days, and I think I've rewritten it about a hundred times." It would be a big financial commitment from the hospital to get this camp started, but conceivably, this camp could draw children from everywhere. In time, if it grew, they would need their own property, their own buildings… Angela stopped herself. It was an enormous dream, and right now she had to concentrate on the first steps necessary to get it started. "And I know the one thing I forgot to mention, which you probably know but I want to state for the record. Walt's going to be there to oversee the medical end of the operation. Helen Baxter, the manager, has given him a room at the lodge so we'll have him whenever we need him." She glanced at Walt Graham, who smiled. "And to begin with, I've got several volunteers who'll be there for various activities. As well as some of the parents."

"How many children?" Fallon Galbraith asked.

"Initially, a dozen. I want a manageable number for starters. Later on, we'll want more, as we take on more staff and know better what will work and what won't. Like I said, we really need this first week to get a good idea of how we're going to operate it over the course."

"Eric and I have discussed it at length, and we think it's a good idea." Neil said. "Part of my brother's endowment was for expansion into new pediatric programs, and I think Gavin would have liked this, and would have been honored to be part of it. But I do have one concern before we agree fully to the camp, and that's the medical end of it. While we know that Walt's a good doctor, we also know that he's had some health concerns of his own lately, and we're wondering if he's going to be able to do all the chasing after the kids that might be required." He deferred to Walt.

"My chasing days are over. But I'll be there to help in any other way I can. Oversee the medical aspects of the program, as we've said. Teach some classes, give some advice. And I've also agreed to do the pre-camp physicals on the children, and have a look at their past medical records to see what we're dealing with. Their insulin dependency, their A1C tests, any other health concerns that might arise." He was the annual Santa on the two-week run of the Christmas train. Twenty-five years in the red suit, twenty-five years with kids of all shapes, sizes and ages sitting on his knee pouring out their fondest wishes. Forty years of bringing babies into this world.

Those things, if nothing else, spoke of his commitment to the children coming to the camp.

"But that still leaves us without an extra chaser," Neil said. "And for this trial run, I want more medical staff on site, since we don't know what we're going to be anticipating. More than that, I want to set up a small clinic, be ready to treat minor emergencies around the clock."

"I'll be glad to volunteer," Fallon Galbraith said. "But I'll need a fair amount of warning as I've got Tyler to take care of." She'd married James Galbraith only a month earlier, and become an instant mom to an active little boy.

"And you know I'm in for whatever you need but, like Fallon, I'll need fair notice, too." James Galbraith was head of Pediatrics at the hospital, and as such on call a good bit of the time.

"I do have one suggestion," Eric said, glancing at Mark.

Mark saw the glance, and shifted his stare to the floor. "And why do I have this feeling that your suggestion has something to do with me?"

"You're not really doing anything yet," Eric said to him.

"Getting ready to start my classes," Mark defended. "You know, those classes you dragged me here to White Elk to teach. Remember? Mountain rescue, *not* kiddie camp."

"Classes that aren't going to start for a few weeks. And at the rate you're dragging your feet selecting your candidates, it could be even longer than that."

"I'm working in Emergency. It's not about dragging my feet, it's about being selective."

"OK, I'll give you that. But you can be selective at camp as well as you can here. And regarding hospital duty, we can schedule around you."

Apparently, that wasn't what Mark wanted to hear because he blew out an impatient sigh. So did Angela and, if anything, hers was louder than Mark's. "I need someone who wants to be there," she said. "It's pretty obvious he doesn't."

"It's not about wanting or not wanting to help the camp. I think it's a worthy cause but that's not why I'm here."

"And he doesn't want to get involved," Angela jumped right in.

In response, Eric glanced over at Neil, smiling as if the decision had been made prior to this meeting. Finalized, approved and stamped.

Mark recognized that. "So I don't have a choice in this, do I?"

Eric didn't even try hiding his growing grin. "Certainly, you have a choice. Just talk to Ed Lester, head of maintenance here, about what you'll need moved up to the lodge for you." He held up his phone. "I've just texted him to get ready, that we'll be doing the moving first thing in the morning. By then Helen Baxter will have your space set aside, and you'll be good to go."

"You've already texted her?" Mark snapped.

Eric nodded. "In anticipation of you accepting the position."

"Oh, and make sure you talk to Marsha Harding, head of Purchasing, about what you'll need in the clinic," Neil added. "She'll have plenty of time to order anything we don't have on hand, and she's expecting your call, too."

Mark glanced at Angela, giving her one of his biggest scowls ever. "Did you plan this? Is that why you wanted me here? To sabotage me this way?"

"Trust me, I'm the one who just got sabotaged. If you think I want to work shoulder to shoulder with you…" She paused, thought back to her dream of only last night, where she and Mark were working shoulder to shoulder, and *she* was in charge. Well, this wasn't what she'd expected, but it did have a certain perverse appeal, she had to admit. "You know, on second thoughts, it'll be fine. Just fine. And I'm sure the children will *love* you."

Mark leaned back in his chair, dropped his head backwards, closed his eyes. Groaned. "When I came here, and *specifically* told you that I didn't want involvement on any level with anything other than the mountain rescue training and maybe some work in Emergency, what was it about that you didn't understand?" His words were meant for Neil and Eric. "What was it about me coming to White Elk that made you think that heaping more and more responsibility on me will change my mind about anything in my life?"

Everybody at the table chuckled. Everybody but Angela, who wondered what could have caused someone with Mark's talent to want to run away the way he was trying to do. Actually, she felt bad for him, felt like she was responsible for trapping him in something he didn't want, and that wasn't her intention. She knew what it was like to be trapped, and wouldn't wish it on anybody. But the choices weren't hers to make. If Neil and Eric thought Mark needed to be at camp as a medic, then he probably did. So now it was up to her to be a little nicer to Mark than she had been. After all, he was now an integral part of the camp's success. The thing was, even with all his medical attributes, she would have been happier with a willing volunteer. And nothing about Mark Anderson was willing. Meaning, in a way, they were both stuck. Only she was stuck in a much better position because, with all her heart, she wanted this to work and he only wanted to get it over with and tick off a few more days on his calendar. "You don't have to be involved," she told him. "Just available."

He opened his eyes, stared at the ceiling for a moment then finally lowered his gaze to her. "Oh, I'll be involved, one way or another. But you're still not getting into my school. That's what this is about, isn't it? You getting a whole week to goad me? Neil and Eric putting us together for an entire week, hoping you'll be able to persuade me? Because they do want you in my program. Won't force the issue but apparently won't drop it either."

"What?" she sputtered, forgetting the audience surrounding her. "Is your ego so inflated that you think my JD camp has *anything* to do with you? Because let me tell you, Dr. Anderson, that nothing is further from the truth. This camp is about the children, and what I'm *not* going to tolerate from you is that attitude. Not around the children. Unleash it on me, let it out in an empty room, take it out on Neil and Eric as they're the ones putting you in this position, I don't care. But *not* around the children."

Chairs at the table scooted across the floor, and Fallon and James exited quietly. So did Dinah and Walt. All unseen to Angela, who was seeing nothing but red.

"And if I could have my choice of a second doctor with me the whole time, it wouldn't be you. Don't flatter yourself into thinking that I begged Neil and Eric to give you to me, because it's their idea, not mine."

"I didn't say *begged*," Mark quipped, biting back a smile.

"Looks like a match made in heaven," Eric commented to Neil.

Angela's attention snapped to her two bosses. "Made in heaven? Do you know how grumpy he is?"

"We know," Neil said, then grinned. "And we're hoping that a week at camp with all those kids might do wonders for his disposition."

With that, Mark shoved his chair back and stood. "I could just walk away, you know. Get in my truck, head down the road, never look back…"

"But you wouldn't," Eric said. "Would you." It was an emphatic statement, not a question. "Because, deep down, that's not who you are."

Angela expected an outburst from Mark, braced herself for it.

Instead, he chuckled. "The best part of having good friends is that they know you. And the worst part of having good friends is that they know you."

"Then you're good with this?" Eric asked. "Because here's the bottom line. If you don't want to do it, if you're totally opposed, we won't force you. We'll find someone else. All you have to do is say the word, and we won't bother you about it again."

"It's a worthy program." He turned, actually bent at the waist in a polite bow to Angela. "My compliments to the director. What you're going to do is a very good thing, and I would be honored to scowl at you every day for a week. And I'll try for a consistent seventy-five percent, Angela." He crossed his heart. "I truly will."

"But I want fifty," she said, relenting into a smile.

Eric and Neil looked at each other, clearly confused.

"Scowling," she explained. "He's only allowed to scowl fifty percent of the time. Oh, and that's around me. Around the children..." She looked pointedly at Mark. "You'll smile. No arguments, no exceptions. When my kids look at you, I want them to see a happy face."

"It's going to your head, isn't it?" he asked. "This position's already going to your head. Or is this payback for you not getting into my class? You're going to torment me for the entire week, torture me into smiling."

To prove his point, he smiled at her. Nice smile, very handsome. Maybe even a little genuine.

Her answer to him was a grin. A great big grin. Then she gathered her papers, stuffed them into her portfolio, and whooshed toward the door. On her way out she stopped, patted Mark on the back and said, "Job well done." Then she went to revise Scotty Baxter's meal plan. It seemed he was substituting cookies for broccoli and ice cream for fruit. A very stubborn little boy. And Mark's first assignment. Somehow she saw the two of them being good for each other.

"She's amazing," Dinah whispered. They were standing over the crib, watching Sarah take a nap. Angela managed to sneak in at least once every hour to visit her daughter, and Dinah came almost as often. "I love my girls, but I've never had a baby, and…"

"And you're still thinking it's time?"

"We are. Eric and I have been talking about it. I think that once Mark gets his program under way, Eric's going to cut back a bit at work. At least, that's the plan."

"But Mark's not going to stay. Won't that put Eric under stress, having to find someone to replace the hightailing Dr. Anderson?"

"Between us, I think Eric's hoping he'll stay. He thinks Mark is one of the most talented doctors he's ever known, and he'd like to have him take over Trauma entirely, which would let Eric get back into pediatric surgery, his first love. And another secret between sisters…I think he and Neil would like to open a separate children's hospital. Or actually turn this one into all pediatrics, and build another one for adult services. Gabby's got her women's hospital, and I think that's been giving them the urge."

"That would be amazing," Angela said.

"And a way off. Which is why we're talking baby sooner rather than later. Because Eric's going to commit himself in other directions, I think, and you know Eric. Once he's committed, he's committed all the way."

"Except Mark isn't going to stay here. That's what he told me. I don't know why he's here in the first place as he seems pretty opposed to it. I don't know what kind of hold

Neil and Eric have on him, but he's made it clear to me that he's counting every one of those days during his eighteen months. And I have an idea that on his last day he'll be out of here like that proverbial shot."

Dinah sighed. "So he says. But Eric and Neil aren't assuming that yet."

"Or maybe that's just wishful thinking." In the crib, Sarah opened her eyes, smiled up at her mother. Then extended her arms into the air to be picked up. "Who could resist that?" Angela said, taking her daughter into her arms. "Did you have a good nap, Sarah?" she asked her.

Sarah, barely a year old, babbled something that Angela took to be a yes.

"Well, Mama has a treat for you back in her office." Her own special blend of natural yogurt, bananas and apricots. "And she has just enough time to give it to you yourself." Even though Sarah was at the age she wanted to feed herself, Angela wasn't ready to give up the experience. She loved it, felt the bonding growing through it. Got sad when she thought of how, in so many ways, her daughter was already finding her own way in life. "And, Dinah, tell Eric to stop talking and start acting. You really do need two or three of these."

"One or two," Dinah corrected, then stepped into the hall.

Angela followed a minute later, after she'd spoken with the head of the nursery, promising her she'd have Sarah back for afternoon playtime. Then she carried her daughter through the main hall, singing Sarah's favorite, "The Wheels on the Bus Go Round and Round…" They passed the conference room, through the hospital lobby, and headed on to the little office adjoining the kitchen. Still singing, still paying more attention to Sarah than to where she was going. Which was why, when she took a sharp turn past the food storage pantry, she nearly crashed into Mark.

"Catchy tune," he quipped, his eyes on Sarah, not on Angela

"Were you looking for me? Because my office isn't exactly convenient to anything else in the hospital unless you're the bread deliveryman."

He held out a pie plate. "Your office was locked. Couldn't leave it inside. Pie was good for a leftover, by the way. Made a pretty good lunch. Definitely something you should consider for your diabetic menu."

"You took half a pie home with you!" she exclaimed, taking a firmer hold on Sarah, who was beginning to squirm.

"And ate it for lunch. It's nice having a homemade meal for a change."

"Pie isn't a meal, and you're not going to eat like that at camp, Mark. Not where I'm trying to train the children to eat proper meals."

"Camp….ah, yes. See, here's the thing. You've got that beautiful little girl. How are you going to be able to leave her behind when you go to camp? Aren't you going to miss her?" He ran a thumb over Sarah's chubby cheek. "Isn't she going to miss you?"

Angela smiled. "You're good, but it's not going to work. Camp is going on as planned, I'll be there, and I'll have plenty of time to spend with my daughter because I've arranged to have her cared for there, the way I have her here, at the hospital, with me. Good try, though. I'll give you credit where it's due."

"Daaa…" Sarah said, looking straight at Mark, holding her arms out to him.

He stepped back.

"I think she wants you to hold her," Angela said, smiling.

"I know what she wants," he said, taking even another step backwards. "And contrary to what she thinks, I'm not her daaa, and I don't hold children unless they have a medical problem."

Not to be daunted, Angela stepped toward him, then lifted Sarah over to him. "I don't like to disappoint her. I'm not sure why she thinks you're her daddy. In fact, I'm surprised she even has the concept of daddy. But she does, and I think you should hold her." She smiled at his distress, smiled even more broadly over the way Sarah was struggling so hard to get into his arms. For whatever reason, her daughter was quite smitten. Briefly, Angela wondered if that was the sign of things to come in the future. Her daughter, and tall, dark, drop-dead gorgeous men?

What was it about Angela? She wasn't merely a little pixie of a woman, she was a huge, overpowering presence. Her entire essence just exploded all over the place, and to be frank about it, it scared him a little. Not because he was anticipating some big love affair with her. Not even because he was anticipating a friendship of more than anything on the surface. But when her *essence* exploded, it got all over people. Caught them up in the same enthusiasm that infected her. And if there was one thing he didn't want, it was enthusiasm, about *anything*.

Still, here he was, sitting in a chair in the worst office he'd ever seen in his life, feeding her baby a yogurt concoction. It was crazy. He wasn't sure how it had happened. One minute he was returning a pie plate and the next he had something sticky spilled on his scrub top because Sarah was fighting him for the spoon, and winning. "You need a better office," he said, holding onto the bowl of yogurt while Sarah also held on, still tussling to get it away from him. Tussling, like mother, like daughter. "And next time bring me a napkin or two."

"Office suits me. It's near the kitchen, I can see the food vendors when they come and go. And even a napkin is a poor defense against Sarah when she wants to be independent." She smiled. "You need a rain slicker."

"What I need is to get back to work." Sarah was too cute. She reminded him of…of things he'd rather forget, things that needed to stay where they were, in the past. He made a move to hand her back to Angela, but Sarah fought him and held on for everything she was worth. And to be honest, he didn't struggle too much to let go. It was nice holding her. If the situation had turned out differently, he might have been a dad to a baby this age.

"She adores you," Angela said. "Just look how happy she is on your lap. I wouldn't want to interrupt her right now. It might affect her digestion. And it's nice just…watching her relate to other people. She's a very friendly little girl."

"What is it about you and your obsession with digestion?" he said, taking his eye off the bowl just long enough for Sarah to grab it and dump it in his lap.

"It's not a bad color on you," Angela said, laughing as she finally rescued Mark by taking Sarah back. "And I'm not really obsessed with digestion so much as concerned by it. Of course, you don't recognize a registered dietician as having any kind of medical expertise…" She put Sarah into a corner playpen and handed her a stuffed bear. Then turned back to Mark. "So explanations would be lost on you."

He stood, walked over to the playpen, bent down and kissed Sarah on the top of her head. "Next time, young lady, we're going to talk about table manners."

Sarah bubbled a little laugh then held her arms out for him again. "Daaa…"

"Mama," he told her. "You want your mama."

Apparently, she didn't. "Daaa…" she persisted.

"You're stubborn," he said, laughing. "Just like your mama."

"And her mama wants to thank you for making the sacrifice."

He gave Sarah's chubby hand a squeeze then turned to Angela. "Sacrifice?"

"The yogurt. Better on you than me."

"Well, like I told your daughter, next time we're having a heart to heart about table manners." What was it about her that made him actually glad he'd come and lost the food fight? It wasn't anything he wanted to think about, or even put away and explore another time. He'd wasted five years with the last woman who'd captivated him, only to discover it had all been a mistake. Of course, killing her father hadn't really helped that debacle of a relationship. But the problem was, he'd bought into all that. Allowed his illusions of what his life should be to cloud his judgment.

That's why he wasn't going to be clouded, ever again. Oh, women were fine for casual companionship, even no-strings affairs. Next time one got herself into a position to persuade him to budge by even a fraction of an inch, though, that's when he was going to turn tail and run. Obligation or no obligation. Friends or no friends. He didn't want the hassle. The truth was, it scared him more now than it ever had, and marriage to Norah Evigan had been a scary situation.

Of course, none of that had anything to do with Angela. For starters, she wasn't his type. Not even close to it. "Esophageal manometry," he said, on his way to the door. "A test used to measure the strength and coordination of the esophagus during swallowing in order to identify the source of problems in the upper digestive system."

As he left, he saw her sit there, arms folded, staring at

him. Probably thinking of ways to best him. Or win what she wanted from him. What he didn't see once he was out in the hall was Angela's mad dash to her little notebook to jot down what he'd just said.

CHAPTER FIVE

"Do you ever relax?" Mark stood off to the side of the hall, Fred tucked under his arm, leaning against the wall, watching Angela literally run circles around him and every other volunteer at the Three Sisters Juvenile Diabetes Boot Camp. She'd been working at this pace for a week now. And that in addition to her duties at the hospital. It seemed like he bumped into her everywhere he went and, to be honest, it was getting to be a little embarrassing. Not because he bumped into her so much but because she did twice as much as anyone else, and twice as fast. On top of that, she baked cookies and brought them to the volunteers almost every day.

And here he was, feeling like the tortoise who *wasn't* going to win the race with the hare.

"At night, with Sarah," she said as she flew by him, pausing briefly to scratch Fred on the head.

Impulsively, he reached out, grabbed her by the arm and stopped her. "This pace isn't good for you, Angela. You need to slow down or it's going to slow you down to a point where you're not able to do anything."

"Why?" she asked, not even trying to disguise her impatience over this distraction. "So you can keep up with me?"

"Ah, yes, I'd almost forgotten the sharp wit of Angela

Blanchard." He chuckled. "I've actually missed it a little this past week, you've been so busy."

"No, you haven't," she said, relaxing a little.

"OK, so maybe I haven't missed the sharp-tongued barbs so much as I've missed the lady who hurls them. But I am serious about the pace you're keeping. Between setting up the lodge for your camp and your job at the hospital…plus those cookies, and did I mention that plain sugar cookies are my favorite? Anyway, you can't keep going like this."

"Is that the doctor speaking, or the man who can't keep up with me?"

Her lips didn't curl into a smile when she said that, but her eyes were a giveaway. They sparkled with a little bit of mischief and a whole lot of…well, the only thing that came to mind was challenge. Challenge, and not in a bad way but in the kind of way that made him want to get to know her a little better. Get to know her outside what he saw. Which was a totally bad idea. "You think I can't keep up with you?"

"Can you?"

Yes, definitely challenge in her eyes. "I've done what I was supposed to. The clinic is set up, I've ordered the supplies I'll be needing. Taken Fred on his fifth walk for the day. Worked with Walt on some medical protocol. Interviewed three candidates for my school. Talked to two parents about your JD camp. Bought a new bag of dog food."

"Simple things, Doctor. That took you, what? Two, maybe three hours? And how long did storytime at the library take you?"

"Damn small town," he grumbled. "Can't do anything here without the whole town talking about it." He'd taken Fred to storytime, not a big deal. "Richard Whetherby asked if I would. Since I wasn't busy at the time…"

She studied him for a moment then conceded victory in this little encounter with a smile. "That's nice, Mark. Let me know when you'll be doing it again, because I'd like to bring Sarah."

"You're assuming that I will?"

"I'm assuming that you won't disappoint the children."

"Too many assumptions are dangerous, Angela," he warned. In truth, he'd already committed to another story-time, then had second thoughts afterwards. Not because of the deed so much as the appearance of establishing ties in White Elk. He didn't want to dig himself in any deeper here, yet that's what he seemed to be doing every time he turned round.

"Dangerous for whom?"

"Look, just tell me what you want me to do now, OK?" No trying to hide the annoyance in his voice. "Give me a list and let me get to it."

"It was a nice thing, Mark. Don't deny yourself the good feelings that come from doing something nice."

"The list?" He held out his hand for it, so she thrust a list at him. Still smiling. Probably sensing his conflict about such a simple thing. Probably appreciating it in some perverse way.

"OK, it's a food order. Delivery's on it's way in right now. You can go to the back door, meet them, check everything off the list and make sure it gets organized in the pantry."

"Organized? How do I do that?"

"I have a list for that, too."

"Of course you do." He glanced at the list in his hand. "And I suppose you'll want me to take the food items I check off from this list and arrange them on the shelves according to your other list. Which makes me curious, Angela. Do you have a list of lists, so you'll know what lists you have to work from and which ones you'll have to create?"

Rather than taking offense, her eyes sparkled. "You know, that's a great idea. I'll put it on my list of things to do."

"Am I on a list somewhere, Angela? One of your things to conquer?"

"Maybe you are."

"Good list, bad list?"

"Let's just call it a perplexing list."

"You think I'm perplexing?"

She nodded. "You do nice things, but you don't want anybody to know it. You're compassionate and you try hard to hide it. You really do want to be involved in worthy causes. Taking care of Fred's a good example of that. But you grumble about it. And you scowl, even though you're really not grumpy. More like preoccupied. Yet you like it that people think you're grumpy and stay away from you. And that, Dr. Anderson, is a very perplexing list."

"And a very boring one. So, on that note, I'll go see if Emoline wants to take Fred home with her tonight, because who knows how long organizing your pantry is going to take? Then I'll excuse myself to the pantry before you come to some kind of screwy conclusion with your psychoanalysis of me. But before I break my back hauling food, there's one condition. And I'm dead serious about this."

She faked a shiver. "I'm not sure I want to find out."

"It's not that bad. It's also in your best interests."

The mischief in her eyes overtook the challenge. "I have a hard time believing that. Especially when I know that you don't even want to be here. So, what is this *one* condition?"

"Dinner."

She blinked. "As in…"

"As in dinner. The two of us, tonight. Or three, if you don't have arrangements made for Sarah." He checked his watch. "Three hours from now. You need the rest, and I think the only way you're going to get it is to either let me sedate you or take you out to dinner. Because, if you really want to give this program your all when it starts in a few days, you're going to have to be rested for it. The children deserve that. And, you deserve, too. So, it's your choice. Sedative or dinner? Oh, and so you won't get the wrong idea, we'll talk about the camp. I have some ideas I want to go over with you, some things I'd like to try doing with the children. Dinner's as good a place as any to talk about it."

"Not a dinner date, but a working dinner?"

"I do work, but I don't do dates. So, yes, a working dinner."

"Can I add that to my perplexing list?"

"Agree to dinner, and you can add anything you want to your list."

She glanced at her own watch then nodded. "OK, then. I'll ask Dinah if she can look after Sarah for me. But let's make it four hours. And I'll cook."

"But I wanted you to relax."

"Cooking is relaxing. And I'm anxious to try out the kitchen here."

"OK, you can cook. But three and a half hours, not four." She actually held out her hand to shake on the deal and when she did, when he took hold and their palms glided over one another's, a little tingle leapt up his arm. From his skin to hers, it was the true jolt out of the blue. One he hadn't expected and, from the look on her face, one she'd also felt and likewise hadn't expected.

"Static electricity," she said, pulling back her hand and wiping it down the leg of her jeans. "Common here, in the winter, when the humidity is low."

"Static electricity," Mark agreed. "Or…" There was nothing to finish that sentence with, because the implication was one he wouldn't consider. Not even with a woman as sexy as Angela. And make no mistake, in her tight little jeans, and that pink sweater she was wearing… "Static electricity," he repeated, trying to snap that last image from his mind.

Twenty minutes later, with Fred on his way to a night of Emoline Putter's pampering, Mark was directing the unloading of food from the delivery truck, trying to keep his mind focused on the various cans, boxes and sacks. But somehow all this food reminded him of Angela. And Angela reminded him of…well, no other woman he'd ever met.

The problem was, with the exception of his ex-wife, who was unforgettable for so many unpleasant reasons, every other woman he'd ever met was *thoroughly* forgettable. Every woman, that was, except Angela. And the fact that he was about to organize cases of canned tuna on shelves for her wasn't good. Not good at all.

"Very nice," Angela said, stepping into the pantry a while later.

"Nice? That's all you've got to say? I've been busting my back for hours, getting everything inventoried off the truck then put away. And I'll have you know, I went by my own list, not yours." To prove it, he held up a sheet of paper covered with illegible scrawls.

"Oh, foolish man, thinking your list can top mine." She arched a critical eyebrow, or tried to, but she couldn't keep a straight face doing it. "Can you even read your list?"

"It's perfectly legible."

She grabbed it from his hands, studied it for a moment then asked, "Looks like doctors' scrawl to me. So, what does it say?"

Grabbing the list back, he looked, frowned, then nodded. "Put the…um…" Frowned again. "Put the mayonnaise on the top shelf."

"Except I didn't have mayonnaise ordered. I make my own—a healthier version than the commercially prepared."

She grinned. "And the only thing I see on the top shelf is rice, which should be on the bottom, as the bags are heavy."

"Rice, olive oil, mayonnaise…" He shrugged. "It's still a perfectly good list, and the proof is in the pantry." He stepped aside to allow her the full view.

Actually, he was right. The proof *was* in the pantry. The shelves were lined up perfectly, and the pantry looked like a small grocery store. Large cans, large jars, large boxes, all, she noticed, with their labels turned facing out. And they were sitting so neatly he could have measured each container's position with a ruler. With the exception of only a couple if things that would have to be rearranged, it was perfect. "You're not compulsive, are you?" she asked, running her fingers lightly over the large jar of gherkins.

"Actually, I'm not the compulsive personality in this room. But I knew that if I didn't get this in good order, the compulsive personality would make me do it over." He grabbed hold of his aching back, faked a scowl. "And I'm too tired, too hungry."

Angela laughed. "Having a little power feels so good."

His response was to twist the jar of gherkins around until the label faced backwards. "Sometimes disrupting the power is good, too."

"You really do like to go against the system, don't you?"

"Mostly when I see that the system needs some going against."

"And you think I need some going against? Is that what this is about?"

"What I think is that *you* think everybody needs some going against. And I'm just imitating the teacher."

That was a fair assessment. She knew that. Recognized it in herself. But in her defense, which she wouldn't say out loud, she'd had to become like that to survive Brad. Loving the wrong person had been so exhausting, and if she'd relaxed, if she hadn't always fought against him so much, well...she wouldn't have come away from him strong. For Sarah, she had to be strong rather then being another one of those casualties who wandered through life never knowing where they were, or who they were. "Sometimes you just have to fight," she said. "It's what makes sense at the time, I suppose."

"But wouldn't it be nice, Angela, being in a place where you didn't have to fight?" His voice was gentle, serious. So much so it sent chills up her spine.

"Are you in that place, Mark?"

She knew he wasn't. The grimness she saw on his face when he wasn't forcing himself to look pleasant said so much.

"The place I'm in is a dark pantry with a pretty lady who prides herself on pushing the wrong buttons."

"So it's OK for you to analyze me, but I can't do the same to you?" She'd come close to touching something deep, possibly the thing that others knew about him but which he'd never told her. In a way, she wanted to know. But in a bigger way, it scared her, because knowing would take their relationship to a different level, and she truly did not want them to go anywhere other than where they were.

"Something like that. And if you could get a clear look at my face right now, you'd see a scowl. But that's because I'm off duty. And that's what I do when I'm off duty. I scowl."

He'd changed the subject, and it was a relief. Now they could get back to their usual level, the one where they tossed barbs back and forth and took care to make sure none of those barbs were truly sharp. Actually, she liked that place. "You've had so much practice doing it, too."

"Angela!" Ed Lester shouted from outside the pantry.

"In here," she called back.

Ed, the head of maintenance at the hospital, poked his

head inside. "Just wanted to tell you that I've got some boxes full of laptop computers. Edith Weston donated them to the program and asked me to bring them up here."

"Put them in the central storage for now," she instructed. Then turned to straighten out the jar of gherkins. When she did, Ed shut the pantry door, which automatically turned off the light.

"So, is this where I asked you if this was planned? You know, you paid him to come and shut us in?"

"Right," Angela said, fumbling along the exterior wall for the light switch. "My true motive was getting you alone in the dark."

"It's happened before," he said, chuckling. "And I wouldn't waste my time on the light switch. It's outside the door."

Angela sighed audibly as she sidestepped over to the door, taking care not to bump into the stacks of boxes along the wall. Thankfully, the little ribbon of light streaming in from under the door was just enough to give her a dim view as her eyes adjusted. "Well, my fondest wish right now is a nice Alfredo sauce. Linguini and crab. A hearts of romaine salad. Not a fumble and tickle among the saltine crackers." She found the door, grasped the handle. Turned it and…

"Let me guess. It's not opening." Mark stepped up closer to her, like that would change the situation.

"It's locked. Probably on the outside, like the light switch is. Who in the world would build a pantry this way? I mean, it's a brand-new construction. They should have known better. Somebody should have…" She jiggled the handle, started to get frantic about it.

Mark laid a hand on her shoulder. "Are you afraid of the dark?"

"No," she snapped.

"Claustrophobic?"

"No!"

"Then calm down, and I'll call someone to come get us." He pulled out his cell phone, flipped it open, and... "No signal."

That triggered her. Not a panic reaction as much as an agitated one. She didn't have time for this. And the heck of it was, if they stayed in there all night, no one would even notice. Dinah wouldn't. In fact, her sister would be thinking all kinds of things...the kinds of things that set Angela pounding on the pantry door. "Help!" she shouted. "Somebody, let us out! We're in the pantry. Let us out!"

Thirty minutes later, her fists were sore, her voice hoarse, and they were still locked in a dark pantry. *Together.* "Any ideas?" she asked, slumping down onto the floor next to him.

"Wait."

"Well, isn't that just helpful!"

"Give me some tools and maybe I can take the door off the hinges. Unless the hinges are on the outside, too."

"Good idea. But I don't have tools." Angela huffed a loud, frustrated sigh. "It's after six. Nobody's here."

"Someone will miss you shortly when you don't show up for Sarah. And they'll come looking. So until then we make the best of it. Relax. Rest. Take a nap...I'll bet you never take a nap, do you?"

"I don't want to take a nap!" Not now, not while she was thinking about the fact that nobody would come looking until morning.

"Suit yourself. But it's awfully tight in here for you to pace, and unless you plan to whip up a miracle dinner in here, that's about all there is to do."

Angela reached over to the shelf, grabbed a bag of pretzels, and thrust it at him. "Here's dinner," she said in a disheartened voice. *"Bon appetit."*

* * *

If it weren't for the fact that the floor was hard and the company was ice cold, it wouldn't have been a truly bad situation. But his back ached from all the physical labor of getting this pantry stocked, and the cement floor underneath him wasn't making him feel any better. Neither was the fact that Angela had been sitting off in the corner for the past hour, totally silent, except for the occasional exasperated sigh. He knew she had things to do. And he'd actually intended to go down to the hospital this evening, after dinner, and put in a shift in Emergency. It wasn't scheduled, but Neil was on and he was sure Neil would have appreciated an evening off to be with his family. Then there was the other thing…he hadn't seen a patient in a week now, and he missed it. Sure, his intention was to leave medicine behind him. So he was surprised that he was actually itching to get back to the ER for a shift.

"What time?" he asked Angela.

"What time, what?"

"Will Dinah or Eric start worrying about you?"

"About seven."

"Then we shouldn't have to wait much longer. It's just after seven, now, so they should come looking pretty soon."

"In the morning. Seven, *in the morning*."

"You're joking, right?"

"Wish I were, but I'm not." He didn't need to know what Dinah hoped they were doing. That would only complicate things. "My sister was going to keep Sarah all night. So…"

"So unless the lodge is haunted and a kindly ghost lets us out, we're here all night."

"All night…"

"Could be worse."

"How?"

"We could be stranded in a cave, or somewhere out in the snow. I've spent some miserable nights out in the mountains, on various rescues. Bad weather. Conditions you can't even imagine. At least here, we have pretzels." He crinkled the bag. "So, let me see if I can feel around for some of that bottled water I brought in, and we'll be set for the night."

"I think I like you better when you're grumpy," she snapped. "At least then I know what to expect from you. But now you're sounding so...so chipper. Like maybe this is what *you* planned."

Mark chuckled. "One of the things I stress in my classes is that you have to make the best of a bad situation. Being grumpy, complaining, pacing, worrying...it all just wears you down, and when you're in a situation you don't want to be in, you really need to keep your focus. So if you let the surrounding elements get to you, you're letting yourself get distracted. And on a rescue you can't let that happen. No exceptions."

"You can actually think that clearly when you find yourself in a bad situation? Say, you're rappelling down the side of a mountain and you get stuck. You're hanging in midair, can't go up, can't go down. Ground's about a mile below you and the top is so far away you can't see it. Can you honestly say that you're not going to get distracted by your situation?"

"You want my lecture on that? Because it's brief and to the point. And what I say will save your life in just that situation."

"Have you been in that situation?"

"Once."

"And you didn't panic."

"I knew what I was doing."

"So give me the lecture. Tell me how you hung up there and didn't get distracted."

"Well, first, it's about the equipment. If you climb a mountain on my time, you use an ATC—that stands for air traffic controller. You use it for both belaying and rappelling because it doesn't kink, it has no moving parts, and it's easier on the hip skin than a hip belay. It's also light, inexpensive and safe if you know how to use it the right way."

"And a belay is?"

"Belaying refers to different techniques used in climbing to apply friction on a climbing rope so that a falling climber doesn't fall too far."

"That's a good thing, I suppose."

"It is, if you're falling."

"And you've fallen?"

"Trust me, I've fallen. And it was long, and painful."

"I get the feeling we're not talking about you falling off a mountain," she said.

"Isn't mountain-climbing an analogy for life? You're either fighting to get to the top, or hoping that once you get there you don't fall off. And one misstep along the way…"

"Spoken like a true cynic…about life, not mountain climbing."

His audible sigh filled the dark room. "Not cynical so much as experienced. Mountain climbing's more predictable than life. If you do everything right, the odds are in your favor. In life, if you do everything right…who the hell knows what happens?"

"That's why you're quitting medicine? Because life isn't predictable?"

"It's as good a reason as any."

"But you're good, Mark. Eric and Neil practically skip up and down the hospital halls singing your praises. And the way you took care of Sarah after the avalanche—"

"Sarah was fine," he interrupted. "Every time you brought her into Emergency, she was perfect."

"OK, then the way you took care of Sarah's mother by indulging her bouts of anxiety when she brought Sarah in to be examined."

He chuckled. "You're a good mother. I worked in a

hospital…one of the largest hospitals in California…and I was confronted by bad mothers all the time. You know, mothers who didn't care, mothers who neglected their children's medical concerns or totally neglected their children. I saw some pretty ugly things when I was there, so there's no way I'm going to fault someone who might have brought her child in a time or two more than was necessary."

"And that's why you're leaving medicine? You burned out because of the bad things you had to deal with?"

"No, those were easy because, no matter how bad the situation, I was taking care of someone who needed help, trying to help them get better. As discouraging as the bad cases can be, I never minded giving the care. But the reason I'm leaving medicine is that in one instance I displayed a gross lack of good judgment and killed my father-in-law."

His words hung heavy in the darkness. So heavy, Angela could barely get her breath. "That's not the end of the story, is it?" she finally managed to ask.

"The story? There is no story. We were on our way home from a banquet honoring my father-in-law. He was retiring as a cardiac surgeon. Well respected, beloved. A little intoxicated. So I drove us home—him, my wife, me. But I wasn't in much better shape to drive than he was. Not intoxicated…I don't indulge. But exhausted. I'd come off of thirty-six straight hours on duty…hard duty, lots of traffic accidents due to heavy fog. And I could barely keep my eyes open. Didn't want to go with my wife and her father in the first place, but… Let's just say that better sense didn't prevail. I went, dozed my way though the banquet and afterwards asked Norah, my wife, to drive when I realized that Tom… my father-in-law wasn't able. But my wife…well, she liked the privileged life and it was always easier for me to let her have her own way. Never seemed worth the effort to argue with her. And that night she was tired, didn't want to drive, so I got behind the wheel. Didn't doze off, mind you. But I was fighting it.

"My reflexes were slow, though. And we were struck broadside by another car. He'd run a stop sign, and if I'd been more alert, I might have seen it coming. But that's something we'll never know. Anyway, I was fine. Suffered a broken shoulder from the seat harness, some air-bag burns, but good. To cut a long story short, my father-in-law died."

"But it was an accident. Not your fault."

"See, that's the thing. It *was* my fault. Maybe not the accident itself. But I'm a trauma surgeon and I failed to see his fatal injuries. Thought he looked fine. Did what he said when he told me to look after Norah first."

"Like any father would do. Mark, I'm so sorry," she whispered, not sure what else there was to say.

"He was a good man. He deserved better than what he got at the end, which was a son-in-law who missed a crucial diagnosis. So anyway, there you have it. I was on my way out the door. Resigned my post at the hospital, and ready to try something different. Then Neil and Eric asked me to come here. " He chuckled bitterly. "They knew exactly what they were doing, telling me they needed help. Friends help. That was the example I'd learned from my father-in-law, and I felt like I owed it to him, as well as to Neil and Eric. They asked for eighteen months, I agreed to it. And I know they're counting on me to stay on when those eighteen months are done. You know, settle in to White Elk, have a change of heart, let those damn Three Sisters work their magic on me, or whatever the hell the legend is. But the thing they don't have to live with, that I do, is the look on my father-in-law's face when he died. He was so shocked. Not frightened, not angry. Just…"

His words trailed off, and Angela wasn't sure what to do. Leave him alone for a while? Comfort him? In the dark, sitting on the cement floor, there weren't many options. "I'm not sure what to say," she finally admitted, "because I don't think words will make you feel better. Time will do that, and in some ways accepting that you're only human will alleviate some of the pain. But right now…"

Mark laughed aloud, breaking the tension. "Isn't this the place where you're supposed to put your arms around me to comfort me, then we…?"

"Have pity sex?" The suggestion as well as the tension breaker caused her to laugh. "Something I learned a long time ago, from my husband, was that sex doesn't make it better if it's not good to begin with."

"And we're not good?"

Actually, they were. Better than she'd thought they ever would be. Although she wasn't going to admit it aloud. Because the truth was she might have been persuaded in amorous ways in that closet, not out of pity but inasmuch as even in the dark, when she closed her eyes, she could picture herself in his arms. And that image caused a raise in her pulse that excited her, yet worried her more than it excited. Her relationship with Brad had started off physically and she'd always thought everything else would catch up to that. But it hadn't. So now she was cautious. Not prudish. Just cautious. It was as simple as that. "So tell me more about belaying," she said, glad to be off the subject.

He chuckled. "You and me both, Angela."

"What's the supposed to mean?"

"I think you know."

She didn't even have to think about it because she did. They were good. And they were both wounded in deep ways. Ways that couldn't be explored or cured in a pantry. In other words, proceed with caution. "Yes, I think I do."

"So…the friction is usually applied by the climber's companion. You never climb alone, by the way. Anyway, it's applied by the companion at the other end of the rope, and it's his job to watch the climber and be ready to jam the rope as soon as he sees the climber fall. What's going to break that fall is that in a typical layout one end of the rope is tied to the climber. It passes through a metal loop fixed into the rock and runs down to a second person, called the belayer. He's the one who stays at the bottom, watching the climber. And he's the one who's wearing a harness to which a ring, called a belay device, is attached. If the climber falls, the belayer locks the rope in the belay device, and the climber's fall is stopped. He's left dangling, probably pretty sore, but he's safe."

"Too bad life doesn't come with a belay device," she said. "Sounds like we could all use one sooner or later." For her, sooner. As in right now!

CHAPTER SIX

"I HOPE that's your elbow," she said, yawning. Punching the glow dial on her watch, she saw that it was definitely morning. Early. Too early to be rescued, though. And the truth of it was she didn't mind being curled up in Mark's arms. It hadn't happened consciously but more out of groggy attempts to find a comfortable position. As it had turned out, her comfortable position was against him, curled up at his side, one arm flung over his chest, her head in the crook of his shoulder.

Amazing, she'd slept well that way. Had listened to him breathe for a while, not sure if he'd been sleeping. Then had dozed off.

"I think it's *your* elbow," he said. "And it's in my ribs."

"I think it's that jar of olives we opened," she mumbled, not ready to move away from him. It was good here. Comfortable in an awkward sort of way. Instinctively, she laid her fingers to his neck and felt the beat of his heart. She'd heard it in his chest, marveled at its strength, and now she was feeling it. And it was so...personal.

"What are you doing?" he asked.

"Taking your pulse."

"OK, I get that. But why?"

"Because I can. I mean, what I'm feeling under my fingertips is your life force. It's a powerful thing. Kind of..."

"What?"

"Sexy, I suppose." She moved her fingers just slightly up his neck, tracing the feel of his heartbeat.

"Well, I've got to tell you that you're the first person I've ever heard call a pulse sexy."

"So maybe not sexy as much as…"

"No! I like sexy."

Angela rolled out of his arms and sat up. It was so tempting to stay there, to think about all the things they could do in the dark, the self-indulgence, the surrendering to temptation. And make no mistake about this. *She was tempted.* Everything about Mark, about this situation, tempted her in ways she'd never known sexual temptation could exist. But if she ever gave in to that, with any man, she wanted it to be…special. She'd missed out on special with Brad. That had been more about convenience…his convenience. Her naivety. Consequently, she just didn't want to do that anymore. Wanted better things for herself now, because whatever touched her touched Sarah. "Care for some water? Pretzels, olives? I think I might be able to find—"

"You're not comfortable with me, are you?" he interrupted. "On a colleague basis, we're OK, but this…it makes you nervous."

"A little." She reached for a bottle of water, not so much because she wanted a drink but because she wanted something in her hands. Something to fidget with. "My marriage was, well, I guess the best thing you could say about it was that it was tolerable most of the time. Brad wasn't around much, so I wasn't being smacked in the face every single day with the things he was doing. I don't suppose I even knew I was living in a delusional world, where everything was the way I wanted it to be, not the way it was. If I'd known all the truth, which I doubt I do even now, I'm not sure how much of a difference it would have made because I don't think I was ready to do anything differently. Not even when I knew he was cheating. Because I repressed myself so I could hang onto him. Although now that I'm away from all that, I can see how I stopped being me in order to have him. Then one day I was too old for him and he told me it was time for me to settle down. Not him, mind you. Me. In other words, he didn't want the *old* wife following him around anymore."

"Old? Had he taken a good look at you? Seriously, any *sane* man would be flattered having you with him."

"That's kind of you to say. But I saw the end coming. It was inevitable. I'd married him in spite of his proclivities, and I would never let myself think past the moment. But then there was Sarah, and everything changed. Well, everything but Brad."

"Let me guess. He didn't want children, you did."

"Yes, I wanted a child, had wanted one for years, but Brad was adamant that he didn't want to be tied down that way. And our relationship was always about what Brad wanted."

"So how did you end up with Sarah?'

"It happened when Brad and I had separated. We'd agreed to go our different ways to see if it worked out. Naturally, for him, it was working out beautifully. For me, not so good. I was so lost. Anyway, he was coaching up in Vancouver, I took a trip up so we could talk, didn't expect that he'd even want to touch an *old* woman like me anymore, so I wasn't using precautions. But apparently he was in the mood for old. Anyway, he moved to White Elk with me for a while, before I found out I was pregnant, but it wasn't enough for him. I wasn't enough for him. And Sarah was too much."

"You're very pragmatic about it," Mark said.

"I spent eight years being pragmatic about my relationship, because that's what I had to be. Otherwise I'd have gone crazy. Or maybe crazier than I already was as I'm the one who kept hanging on for so long." She opened the bottle of water and took a drink. Her throat was dry, probably from so many revelations. The truth was, he was easy to talk to. She wasn't much of a talker, though. Not when it came to the messes of her life. Because, to other people, what she'd done looked foolish. Probably because it was. So she'd learned a long time ago that the saga of her ill-fitting marriage really wasn't a topic for discussion. Certainly not with strangers. And while Mark wasn't exactly a stranger, he wasn't *not* a stranger either. Which made her need to unburden herself seem even more unusual.

But he was a good listener. Said just the right words in the right places. The kind of man she should have chased for all those years, rather than the one she had. "I didn't mean to do that."

"What? Tell me about your life?"

"It's not interesting. I did dumb things."

"Love can do that to you. And I'm pretty damned guilty of some dumb things myself."

"Bad marriage?"

"Wrong marriage. I loved her father and believed marrying his daughter would be everything I wanted. He thought we'd be a perfect couple, kept telling me he couldn't wait to welcome me into his family as a son. I was the son who needed a father, he was the father who wanted a son... The funny thing was, as well as I knew Tom, I'd never been around Norah that much. She was always away at school, or traveling. On her brief visits home, she seemed nice. You know, I don't even recall spending much time alone with her. There was no...courtship. She adored her father, so did I, and I think we simply married to please him. It seems crazy now, but at the time it seemed to make sense."

"Was it ever good between you?"

"Maybe at the start. But the more she wanted, the less I was able to give. And I'll take my share of the blame. I was at the end of my residency, starting my new career, I didn't have time for her and she was definitely high maintenance. We didn't have anything in common except her father, and that's not enough to sustain a marriage. Of course, letting him die the way I did…" He paused, his voice broke.

Instinctively, Angela reached out and took his hand. "Why is it that those who are the hardest on us are ourselves?"

"Because, deep down, we know how bad we really are."

She liked the feel of his hand. Soft. Strong. It wrapped around hers like a glove made to fit, and she was in no hurry to break the contact. "You're not bad, Mark. What happened was a tragedy. You had a hard choice to make."

He shoved her hand away. "And made the wrong one. Which is why I shouldn't be heading this mountain rescue program. What you do out there in the field is all about making choices, the right choices. But I've proven myself there, haven't I?"

"That's exactly why you should be the one in charge, because you care so deeply."

"Too damn bad," he said.

"What?"

"That I can't let you into the program."

"I know," she said. "I'm not qualified. I get it. You don't have to keep reminding me. But you're not going to stop me, Mark. I am going to do this, am going to get my certificate, either from you or the next instructor in the door."

"I know you will," he said. Then leaned over and brushed a modest kiss on her cheek.

"What's that for?" she asked, reaching up to feel the warmth his lips had left on her flesh.

"For thinking my pulse is sexy."

It was hard to believe that it had been a week since that night in the closet, but it had been a week, to the day, and neither of them had mentioned it. If he'd been a betting man, he'd have bet that the definite lack of Angela these past seven days had been by design. Her design. They'd passed in the hall, greeted each other cordially, spoken only when necessary, and usually when in a crowd.

It was for the best, he decided. Because he'd enjoyed the way she felt, sleeping in his arms. He'd listened to her breathe for quite a while, not sure if she'd been sleeping or awake, quite enjoying the feel of her, the scent of her. Subtle, earthy. He'd tried to identify the faint whiff of fragrance, and decided to call it Angela, because that was the lingering scent of her, and he'd noticed it before. Liked it. Found it oddly... arousing.

"I've got emergency duty in the hospital," he said, as she whooshed by him in the corridor. "I'll be back by early evening."

She stopped abruptly. Paused a moment. Spun round. "But the children start arriving this afternoon."

"Walt's here, if you need him."

Angela huffed out an impatient sigh. "You know how important this first day is, Mark. I'd hoped... No, never mind. If they need you in the emergency room, that's where you've got to be. So, go!" She spun back round, started to sprint away. But Mark caught up to her, grabbed her by the arm, held onto her.

"What's going on here, Angela? I thought we were doing better together. But we're back to this...this separation. Only there's no bickering. And if we're not bickering, that means we're having problems. Only thing is, I don't know what those problems are. Don't have a clue. Haven't been able to ask because you've been avoiding me. Or approaching me only when you're in a group. So, tell me. Did I mutter something indecent in my sleep? Or grope you without knowing it? Because you've been acting like I have."

"Not here," she muttered, looking up and down the hall at all the people who were stopping by to help with opening day. "Not now!"

"Then tell me when, because I want to get this settled between us. We're going to be spending the next week living at pretty close quarters, and the prospect of spending that with an iceberg isn't very appealing." He wasn't angry. Just perplexed. Especially as they hadn't stepped over the line—a line that had stretched thinner by the minute that night in the pantry. A line that had almost snapped after she'd snuggled into him and had felt so good there he'd fought off sleep just so he could lie in the dark and enjoy the sensation.

"Look, Mark. It's not you. It's me. I'm just not…comfortable in an up-close and personal situation. Not anymore. I proved myself once. Proved just how bad I am at those kinds of decisions, and wasted a lot of years not learning my lessons, even though I was being slapped by them every time I turned round. Since then I just…"

"Don't trust men?" he interrupted.

"Not men, exactly."

"Me? You don't trust me? What the hell did I ever do to you to deserve that?" He growled the words, anger finally beginning to overtake him. He wasn't looking for a lifetime commitment, wasn't even looking for a fling. Just a…well, he wasn't sure what he wanted from Angela. Whatever it was, though, was sure better than what he was getting.

She sighed. 'Look, the truth is you…you remind me of my ex-husband. Not in your looks. But in other ways. Brad is… he's the kind of man women just want to be around. They feel good with him. Safe, protected. They feel like that's where they have to be, or their heart will break."

The scowl on his face softened. The building anger dissipated. "You think that's me?"

She nodded. "You do have that effect. The women at the

hospital talk about you. I see the way they stare at you. You're that lone figure, the one who stands off by himself looking detached and inaccessible, the one they want to persuade, or convert, so to speak. And I just can't..." She stopped, shook her head.

He chuckled. "That's me? That really how you see me?"

"It is."

"I think I'm flattered. In fact, that's just about the nicest thing anybody has ever said about me."

"See, that's just the way Brad would have reacted. Just the thing he would have said."

"Is it really, Angela? Or is it what you *want* to see? Because seeing that in me, or any other man, protects you from making another mistake. You know, judge him to be like your ex, then run away before you allow yourself the chance to find out for sure."

"I don't want an involvement on that level, Mark. Don't want to get close enough to find out if he's really like Brad or if it's my defense mechanism kicking in. Either way, it doesn't matter so long as I keep my distance."

"Then that makes you the lone figure, the one who stands off by herself looking detached and inaccessible. Except that's not really you. I've seen you with Sarah, and when you're with her, when you just look at her...that's who you are, Angela. It's all right there to see. I have an idea. Tonight, after we get all the kids tucked in, come to my room."

She raised her eyebrows, started to back away from him.

"Bring Sarah," he said hastily. "I know it'll be well past her bedtime, but she can sleep in my room. And this won't take long."

"I don't know..."

"Do it, Angela. Trust yourself. Hell, trust me."

Trust him. She did, actually. The one she didn't trust was herself. Because she'd allowed herself to feel good that night in his arms. She'd allowed herself to feel so many feelings she'd never felt in her years with Brad. But the thing was, even if it weren't difficult for her to get involved, there was still Mark and his problems to consider. He was running. White Elk was merely a temporary stop and he was marking off his days. So, even if she did think that she could get involved again, could allow herself to have feelings again, it couldn't be with Mark. He would surely be another heartbreaker, and one broken heart in a life was enough. Next time she wanted stability. No, she demanded stability. And Mark couldn't give it. *Wouldn't* give it, by his own admission.

"Well, the first one's here," Walt Graham said.

Walt was standing at the lodge's large picture window, looking proper and well clipped. Beard neatly trimmed now, making him not so Santa-like. Hair cut short. Nice sweater. He needed a pipe, though not to smoke since Walt didn't smoke. But one for image. Being in love again was doing great things for him. Angela was truly happy for Walt and Catie. A little wistful, too. But maybe someday, for her...

"And I suppose we're ready."

"Nothing to worry about," Walt assured her. "You've done everything you needed to do. Probably more than was necessary. So now let yourself have some fun with this. You need to make sure this is a good experience for you, too, Angela."

"It's all been good so far. But...I guess I'm feeling overwhelmed. It wasn't that long ago I was a cook..."

"Executive chef," he corrected.

"A cook by any other name. Anyway, I was a *chef*. If I made a bad meal, I threw it away. But now, seeing these kids walking up to the entrance, I'm only just now realizing that this is so…" She grappled for words, on the verge of tears. "It's important, Walt. We have to shape the lives of these kids, teach them how to take responsibility for their health, and I'm wondering if I'm really the one to be doing this."

"You'll save lives, Angela. I know how badly you want to be a medic, but this will save lives. You'll train countless kiddies how to be fit, how to eat right, and it's a lesson that will stay with them for the rest of their lives. It's a good thing you're doing here, and because the passion to create this was yours, you'll find the heart to carry it through, jitters and all. I'm sure of that."

Angela ran over to Walt and gave him a big hug. "If Catie didn't already have her eye on you, I'd take you myself," she said.

"Two master chefs wanting the likes of me, and me watching my diet now…a man's fondest dream and worst nightmare."

"I'm glad she got you, Walt. You needed to be gotten."

"So do you, Angela. It's time for you, too. And I've seen the way Mark Anderson watches you. Makes me think it might be time for him as well."

"And women trusted you to deliver their babies?"

"What do you mean by that?" he asked, arching bushy gray eyebrows to reveal twinkling blue eyes.

"You were observant enough to know when a baby was suppose to make its way into the world, yet what you're observing with Mark, and with me…it isn't there. He isn't looking at me *any* way. Except maybe with a little anger or contempt sometimes, since we do have this way of coming at each other."

"See it for what you want, Angela. But I see it for what it is." He waved to the first two children in the doorway.

Emoline Putters, from the hospital, sprang up from behind the hotel desk and welcomed the children in, took their names, handed them information packets with their room assignments which, as it turned out, were two of the large meeting rooms, both decked out with cots, much the way any camp would be. One room for the boys, one for the girls. Better to keep an eye on the kids this way. By the time Emoline had given her first round of directions, the next few children had wandered in, followed by several more, until, finally, all twelve were checked in and being escorted to their rooms by volunteers who'd come to help.

"It's amazing," Gabby Ranard cried, following the children. She was with Neil, Eric and Dinah, who'd all come to watch the launch of Angela's camp. "I knew you could do it, but you've brought it about so quickly, and so thoroughly. Makes me think I should offer you an administrative job in my hospital."

Neil gave his wife a playful nudge. "Don't even try it. She's right where she belongs, and she's not going anywhere." He looked at Angela. "Are you?"

Actually, she still wasn't sure she was there. She needed someone to pinch her. "I'm good," she said, looking past the group to see if Mark had, by chance, wandered in. But he hadn't, and she was oddly disappointed. "Look, I'm going to start orientation in ten minutes, give the kids their instructions, answer questions. Parents will be staying for that, and for lunch, too. So you're all invited. After lunch, though, I'm going to close the camp to all visitors for the rest of the day so everybody can settle in, get used to the place. Settle in without being *observed*. But until then…" She stepped back, extended her hand to show the way down the hall, and smiled. "Welcome to the official opening of the Three Sisters Juvenile Diabetes Boot Camp. Look around, make yourselves at home. Have fun."

"You did a good thing," Dinah whispered to Eric as they wandered off in the direction of the room where orientation would be held. "Not just because she's my sister but because of…all this. Look what she's done here." Dinah swiped at the tears trickling down her cheeks. "My sister *did* all this."

Eric kissed his wife affectionately on the cheek. "I do have quite a knack for recognizing beautiful women with amazing talent, don't I?"

"Can't find anything wrong. Not even a little cold." Mark glanced down at the chart, causing his glasses to slip a little. When he looked back up at Karen Landry, he did so over the tops of his glasses. "Any other questions or concerns?"

"Can you stop by to see her later? I get so worried, Doctor, being alone now, the way I am, with a child to take care of. And the two of us living so far away, as we do."

It was an obvious flirtation. Even as out of practice as he was, he recognized the batting of the eyelashes. And what surprised him was just how impervious he was. Karen Landry was, by all estimations, a looker in every way a man liked to look. All that, plus recently divorced. And this was the third time in two weeks she'd dragged her daughter, Aimee, into Emergency. Coincidentally, always coinciding with the shifts he worked. Her attention was flattering. What red-blooded man wouldn't be flattered by the attention of a beautiful blonde, especially with curves like Karen had? Yet, the harder she flirted, the more he wished it was Angela there, doing the flirting.

Somehow, though, he doubted Angela ever flirted. She ran head first into everything she wanted, and never flirted around the edges of it the way Karen Landry was doing. Which, actually, was a little annoying, come to think of it. "As a matter of fact, I'm tied up at Juniper Ridge Lodge after I leave here. We're opening a camp for children with diabetes, and I'm the doctor on call."

"We're close to Juniper Lodge. Maybe I could bring Aimee *there* to see you?"

Such hope in the woman's eyes. And for a man who didn't want to see hope for him in any woman's eyes. Not ever again. "I'm afraid my duties there will keep me busy. But if you're worried about Aimee again, feel free to come back here to the hospital. We've always got good doctors here in Emergency."

"Should she be tested for diabetes? Maybe I should bring her over to the camp to be tested?"

He looked down at Aimee, who, at age five, had no idea how her mother was trying to use her as a means to wiggle her way into a date, or an affair, or whatever it was that Karen Landry had in mind. He didn't fault Karen, didn't blame her, didn't condemn her. Being lonely was a terrible thing. *He knew.* And he admired the spirit that drove someone to solve that loneliness. Hoped Karen found someone to solve it for her. "Aimee's perfectly healthy. No symptoms of diabetes, no real reason to suspect it. But if you're worried, I'd suggest you call and make an appointment at the children's clinic, and they can get you scheduled in for a full checkup as well as the blood work we'll need in order to make a proper diagnosis."

All the hopefulness on Karen's face sank into despair. "She does eat too many sweets."

"It's not what she eats so much as the way her body metabolizes it. Diabetes is a result of a malfunction in the pancreas." Simple explanation. He hoped it would suffice.

"And you've checked her pancreas? Because if she needs to go to that camp…"

Mark took off his glasses, folded them, put them in his lab coat pocket. "Aimee's fine," he said, trying to sound sympathetic. The truth was, while he felt sorry for Aimee's mother, the fact that she used her child to get through his door wasn't good, no matter what her reason. "There's nothing wrong with her. And for future reference, I won't be seeing Aimee again. All of the other doctors here are qualified to give her all the care she needs, but I'll be withdrawing from practice shortly, and I just wanted to let you know."

"Which doctors?"

"Ranard, Ramsey, Galbraith…" He watched her face turn into a scowl. All were married, which didn't suit Karen Landry's purpose. "And you, Aimee…take care of yourself!" He didn't give candy, but kids liked stickers, he'd discovered. Bright, shiny stickers, and he just happened to have a sheet of them in his pocket for Aimee.

"I will," she promised, reaching out for her stickers.

Such a simple thing to make a child's eyes light up, the way Aimee's were. To be honest, it tugged at his heart a little. So did Sarah Blanchard. Which wasn't a good thing, because those were the longings he had to subdue. They'd almost killed him once and he wasn't going there again. Not for a very long time. If ever.

He watched Karen lead Aimee down the hall to the exit. She wasn't mean to Aimee, but she wasn't attentive. Didn't hold her hand, didn't keep a close eye on her. Didn't look at her with a heart full of love, the way Angela looked at Sarah. With Angela, it was all there to see. Nothing hidden. Her daughter was her entire world. With Karen, though, her daughter was merely a tag-along.

On impulse, he flipped open his cell phone. "I'd like to order some flowers," he said.

CHAPTER SEVEN

"You sent me flowers?"

Mark shrugged. "For your opening day. It's customary when someone opens a new venture."

Angela looked at the bouquet. It was beautiful. Two dozen white roses in a crystal vase. She'd set them on the front desk of the lodge for everyone to enjoy. But kept the card to herself. It wasn't sentimental, but in a way it was. *May all your endeavors be successful.* And it was signed, *Mark.* No love. Just *Mark.* But she wasn't disappointed at all. *Love, Mark* would have complicated things she didn't want complicated. "No one's ever sent me flowers before. I...I don't know what to say."

"Never?"

She shook her head. Then turned to sniff the fragrance. "Brad wasn't very sentimental or romantic. And before him... boys. Mere boys."

"Well, I'm glad I was the first." He glanced at his watch. "Look, I've got to go. Walt and I are teaching a class on, well, the pancreas and the production of insulin." He thought back to Karen for a moment, almost shuddered. "Basic stuff, just to get the kids familiar with the anatomy of their problem."

Angela nodded. "A good place to start."

"So, how's it been for you so far?"

"Pretty good. We had orientation, then lunch. Shooed

the parents out of here then took a tour of the areas where we're allowed. Sent Ed Lester around to lock doors where we aren't. Then went outside and had a look at the beginner slope. Threw some snowballs, did a little sledding…typical snow activities. So now they'll be nice and relaxed, and ready to learn."

He smiled. "Kids absorb information amazingly well. I think a lot of people tend to underestimate them, but if you reach them on their own level, and you're straightforward about doing it, they get it. Sometimes better than we do."

"No wonder Sarah looks at you with such amazement. She gets *you*, I think."

"Mrs. Blanchard!" Harry, a curly-haired child standing at the other end of the hall, called. "Can we go play in the snow again?"

"Looks like your public awaits," Mark said.

"Actually, that's *your* public as it's time to go tell them about the mysteries of the pancreas."

"Insulin," he said.

"What?"

"Insulin, from the Latin *insula*, meaning—"

"Island," she piped up. "Also, insular, a derivative, meaning characteristic of an isolated people."

"Are you accusing me of being insular?" he asked.

"Earlier, I might have. But insular people don't send flowers, do they?" She wasn't going to read anything into the flowers other than a gesture of friendship. At least, she was going to try not to. But the gesture scared her a little. It also flattered her a lot, although more than anything it simply made her happy.

"Some insular people do," he replied.

"Can we go outside, Mrs. Blanchard?" Harry persisted.

"But some insular people, who *think* they're insular, really aren't." With that, she spun round and trotted after the little boy, who was already heading out the door.

"Sarah, how nice your mother came with you this evening." Sarah was already holding out her arms to Mark when he took her from Angela. "Don't tell your mother, but inviting her here was just an excuse to get to see you." He held her on his hip like a natural, but Sarah got other ideas immediately when she saw the pile of stuffed toys on a soft pink blanket on the floor. Immediately, she started squirming to get down.

"You bought those for her?" Angela asked.

"Eric's sister has that boutique in town, Handmade for Baby. Everything guaranteed to be non-allergenic and eco-friendly."

"But so many? There must be ten—"

"Eleven," he interrupted. "Couldn't choose between them, so I bought them all. Figured Sarah would figure out what ones she likes and the rest I'll donate to the hospital." He set her down among the stuffed bunnies and giraffes.

"I think my daughter is going to like all of them."

Mark didn't answer for a moment. Just stood there and stared at Sarah sitting in the stack of animals, looking wide-eyed at them. "I hope she does," he said, his voice a little gravelly. He cleared his throat then faced Angela. "A young lady can never have too many stuffed animals, can she?"

"You're a real softy, you know that?" So much so she was tempted to kiss him. But she didn't. "So, what's this about?" she asked, walking over to the picture window and almost having her breath ripped out of her, the view of sunset on the Three Sisters was so stunning. The golds and pinks settling over the sisters, with the midnight blue closing in around them, and just a hint of lighter blue in the background... White Elk, these mountains...it was home. It was her heart, partly because she loved the people here, partly because this was the first place where she'd ever been truly happy. But mostly because of Sarah. She glanced over at her daughter, who'd latched onto a white dolphin and seemed to be deep in conversation with it. *This* is where she had to raise Sarah, had to give her the opportunity to find the same happiness she was finding here. "Is this the reason?" she asked, not willing to blink for fear she'd miss a second of the sunset.

"It is nice. But, no. I had something else in mind."

That heightened her interest. She turned slowly, not sure what to expect. Only to find… "A rope?" He was holding a length of rather substantial rope.

"I thought I'd teach you how to harness up. Since we talked about it a little the other day, I decided to go buy some equipment and let you see how it feels to put it on."

Well, it was a good thing she wasn't expecting anything romantic, because there was certainly nothing romantic about this. He had equipment…things she didn't recognize, things she guessed he was about to put on her. Which, come to think about it, wasn't a bad way to spend the evening. It got her closer to her goal, and that was a good thing. It also kept her from having crazy thoughts about Mark, and she'd had a few of those recently. Like what would it be like to have him stay in White Elk? Her daydreams really didn't extend into any kind of happily-ever-after scenario because she already knew the end of the story—her staying, him leaving. Still, she'd let her mind wander off to a place where he wasn't anxious to leave, and it was a nice place. A place she thought she might like to be. "You bought this all for me?"

"You seemed interested."

"I am! I mean, I want to learn how to climb. And I want to be good at it. I'm just surprised that… Well, let's just say that this is the last thing I expected. When you asked me here…"

"You thought I would seduce you?" He arched his

eyebrows, showing off the twinkle in his eyes. Then nodded toward Sarah, who'd chosen a polar bear as a pillow and had already gone to sleep.

"You told me to bring Sarah, so I knew that wasn't it. And I'm not sure what I thought. OK?" Actually, she'd played out the scenario ten different ways in her head, yet still hadn't come close to this. And it wasn't about the actual act of teaching her to harness up so much as it was how Mark was going to teach her one of the skills she'd have learned in his school. He wouldn't let her in but, in a way, he was telling her she was worth teaching. He was showing faith in her and that was almost as good as seduction. In some ways, maybe it was better because in teaching her Mark was telling her she was good enough. "But this is good. Really good. So, show me the ropes."

"You're an interesting woman, Angela Blanchard. Seduced by the ropes but not be me?"

"In the future, the ropes will have a place in my life. You won't."

"That's blunt."

"But true." She arched challenging eyebrows. "Can't deny it, Mark."

He laughed. "Let's take this to the other room. I don't want to disturb Sarah."

The other room was smaller, had a desk, a chair, and a mini-kitchen. No bed, thank heavens, because she knew that while seduction wasn't the fare *du soir*, the bed would have been distracting. "So, I've got the rope, now what?"

"Well, the first thing you have to do is with your harness." He handed it to her slowly, let his hand linger on the harness as she took hold of it. "Hold it up in front of you and untangle it. The easiest way to avoid tangling your rope is to make sure you keep it untangled when you put it away. Nothing is more annoying than dealing with a tangled rope." He finally let go of the harness and in doing so, massaged a soft trail over the back of her hand.

Angela sucked in a sharp breath, trying to refocus through the tingles he was causing. "I'll remember that," she said after his hand finally slipped away from her. "No t-tangles."

He nodded. "There are ways to coil a rope, but we'll save that for another day."

Was he purposely sounding seductive, or was she truly in the mood to be seduced? Because the thought of coiling rope with him made her want to do it now, made her ache to do it. The thought of coiling anything with him made her ache in ways she'd never ached before. "Just tell me when," she managed to say without her voice sounding too husky from want. But that was a struggle because she was succumbing to a seduction in which Mark was clearly *not* involved. A seduction all in her head. "So, what comes next?"

"You have to identify the front and back of the harness, as well as the left and right leg loops. Be careful there are no twists in the harness, then put it on around your waist, and make sure it's snug when you buckle it."

It looked simple enough, but it was good to have Mark there to steady her as she yanked the harness into place. "It's not going to be comfortable, is it?" she said, trying to draw the webbing tighter around her waist.

He chuckled. "Not going to be pretty either. But you'll get used to it if you do it often enough. So now that you've got your waist taken care of, do the same for your leg loops. Pull each one around your thigh, and make sure you get them as high on your leg as you can. Then buckle them tight without cutting off your circulation."

She attempted to cinch the left leg first, but Mark stopped her by taking hold of her leg loop and putting it in her hand. Transferring the belt from his hand to hers turned into a lingering touch, one that lasted far too long for anything professional, or even instructional. His touch was on the verge of a caress… Or was it her imagination? She glanced up at him quickly, to see the expression on his face, and for a flash she thought she saw… No, it was definitely her imagination. He was concentrating, almost scowling. "So I, um…I fasten the leg loop around my thigh, and…"

He cleared his throat. "Once around, then double it back. Both legs. And do the same for your waist. Make sure you pay attention to the buckle, though. This harness says *Warning* on each of the buckles, and when you can still see that exposed, you know you haven't doubled back. Also, get in the habit of looking at the buckle. They don't all have the warning. But when you haven't doubled back, it looks like an O. It will look like a C when you've done it properly. And the belay…" He pointed to the front loop. "You've got it twisted. It goes right over your belly button." Maneuvering the harness a bit, his hand rubbed over her belly as he placed the belay over her bellybutton. A touch to send shockwaves thought her body, it was so sensual, so personal, even fully clothed as she was.

Everything inside her braced for the smile she forced, trying to make it look steady while she was feeling jittery. "I remember belay."

"It's important," he said.

Was he sounding awkward? Was this closeness getting to him? Or was it her own nervousness making him nervous? "As in a lifesaver. I learn my lessons well, Doctor." She worked with the belt, got it positioned properly around her waist just fine, but she fumbled doubling the belt back through the buckle. The webbing was stiff and, admittedly, her fingers were trembling a little. "A little clumsy," she conceded, giving it a second try.

Midway through, he took over. "If you're not used to getting this set up, it can be a little tough. And this part is important. You absolutely have to have your double-back done properly, because that's what will hold you in place if you should fall off a cliff. So what you do is…" His fingers brushed over hers again as he took the belt from her. "Push it through the buckle…"

She inhaled the masculine scent of him. Let herself get lost in it. Shut her eyes, enjoying the closeness, enjoying the feel of him. Held her breath to hold in the essence.

"Then pull it back, tight. Can you breathe?" he asked.

Reluctantly, she released her breath. "I'm fine. Just…concentrating." It was crazy, how aroused she was by this. But the goose bumps were rioting now, and his touch was making her legs feel all rubbery.

"Good. Because you need to do the same thing with each of your leg loops. Just double back like we did to your waist. And keep the loops as high as you can. Right up to your…"

She nodded. "As high as it will go."

He nodded back.

She saw little beads of perspiration beginning to dot his brow.

"The webbing on the leg loops is probably stiff, too, so…"

Angela swallowed hard, and forced her concentration to the leg loops. *The leg loops!* She had to get this right. Couldn't be distracted. Couldn't let the skittish lump in her throat pull her out of the task, out of the moment, because this was the instruction she needed. It was about getting her certificate. About so many important things in her life. "It won't loop back through," she said, pulling on the end of the webbing, trying to force it back through the buckle. "I can't seem to…"

"Work with the webbing a little before we do this again. Make it more pliable."

He wasn't going to help her? Wasn't going to finish this

lesson? "Pliable," she mumbled, not ready, yet, to quit. "For the sake of the lesson, can we move on to the next step even though I can't get the leg loops tight enough? As long as I know I have to do it, it shouldn't make a difference if they're loose."

"When you put on your harness, you put it on correctly, no matter what the reason. No exception."

She huffed out an impatient sigh. Impatient at herself for not being able to do this simple task. Impatient with him for being so rigid about it. "Then I guess we're through for the evening, because I can't get the webbing to double back through the buckle."

As if trying to figure out what he wanted to do, Mark shut his eyes for a moment. Was he being impatient with her? Or sorry he'd started this, because she'd failed at such a simple thing? Buying this equipment and trying to teach her had been a nice thing to do. Unexpected. So, was he regretting it now?

Without further thought, she decided he probably was, which meant it was time to leave. Time to get Sarah, take her back to their suite where Edith Weston would sit with her, then go and fix evening snacks and have a late-night session with the kids about how blood sugar can either spike or bottom out over the course of the night, depending on what they ate during the evening. But she was *so* not in the mood. Not in the mood to do anything but return to her room, hold Sarah, and remember that everything she was doing was for her daughter. Refocus on that! "Look, I appreciate the lesson, but since it doesn't look like we're going to be able to go any further than where we are…"

Suddenly, he had the belt of the leg loop in his hand, doubling it back through the buckle. Once it was adjusted, he slipped his hand between her thigh and the belt. "No more than a hand's thickness. Anything looser is wrong."

The feel of his hand on her thigh caused her to gasp. "You…you startled me," she lied. For, he hadn't startled her at all. But if he moved his hand another inch up, what he might do would surely rouse a gasp even louder than the one she'd just let out.

"You've got to get it right, Angela. If you don't, you could fall out of your harness if you flip upside down."

She was definitely flipping upside down now, just not in the way he defined it. "Upside down is…" This time, as he adjusted her other leg loop then tested it for proper tightness, she didn't gasp. She merely sighed. Then looked up at him, met his eyes, saw the same fire there she knew was in her own. "Mark, I, um…we…"

The moment of decision wasn't prolonged. Mark leaned in and brushed his warm lips to Angela's, as his hand reached to caress her cheek. At first, Angela was dazed by his touch, dazed by her need for it, and she didn't respond to the tender kisses he was giving. She merely lingered there, enjoying them, reveling in them, imprinting them in her mind, her heart. But all too soon his tender kisses turned demanding, seeking her response. She moaned softly, low. Or maybe the moan was his. It didn't matter. Nothing mattered as gentleness turned into passion, and she licked her tongue across his lips, drawing out a moan that was most definitely his.

His moan startled her, woke her from her daze, caused her to break apart from him. But what she couldn't break was his stare…the longing, the raw need. "Mark, I think…"

He shushed her, reaching out his hand and running his thumb over her lips. Brushing them lightly. Causing a tingle so sensual all she could do was close her eyes for the moment, and allow it. Allow Mark. Allow anything. "It probably isn't a good idea, is it? Not with Sarah in the next room. Not with all the kids down the hall," he said, as his fingers moved up her cheek and entwined in her short hair, giving it a playful little tug.

Were his fingers trembling a little? Or were her nerves so unraveled that it was she who was shaking? "No, it's not," she murmured, so enjoying his feathery caress that she regretted having to stop. "I haven't been with anyone. Nothing. Not for a long time," she told him.

"I understand," he said, moving his thumb back to her lips.

Which was fast becoming her favorite sensation in the world. She tilted her face up to look at him and their lips met again, but this time with all the force she could find in herself. Curling her fingers around his neck, she pulled his head toward her, demanding more ardent kisses. Their tongues danced together and in unison their breaths quickened. Mark raised his hand, slipped it alongside Angela's neck for a moment, then all restraint was lost. He crushed her hard to his chest, and the kiss was as exacting as everything else about him was. Firm, forceful, both of them giving, both of them greedy to take. It was their essence, the soul of their relationship, the kiss of the adversary finding its rightful place. And in a heartbeat Angela stopped. Looked at the buckle. Saw the word. The one word that said everything. *Warning.*

"It's not about Sarah, and not about the kids down the hall. It's about my plan," she whispered, too stunned by what she'd come so close to doing that her voice hadn't yet found its way back to her. "*You're* not in my plan." She looked up at him. "Don't you see? This can't happen. Not now. Not… us." She took another step backwards.

"You think something was going to happen?" he asked. His voice was curt, and the scowl on his face as deep as she'd ever seen it. "It was just…" He shook his head. "Whatever it was. Nothing."

Nothing? It was nothing to him? Suddenly, she knew why she couldn't do this. Why she'd promised herself she wouldn't. She could feel the little rent in her heart. The small crack that would have surely turned into deep heartbreak had the kiss gone on much longer. She was falling in love with this man. Fighting against it with everything she had in her, and failing anyway. Oh, she knew better. But the feeling wasn't entirely hers to control. And he'd done what she'd known all along would happen. "Nothing," she said. "You're right. It was nothing."

She turned, fought against the urge to run away, and mustered all the dignity she could find. Still cinched in her harness, its straps dangling everywhere, she walked into the other room, picked up Sarah, then walked to the door. Once there, she turned back to him. "I appreciate the lesson, Mark. I hope we can get past this…this *nothing*, so you can teach me the next part of it."

He didn't say yes. Didn't said no either. In fact, he said nothing. And once she was in the hall, she hurried to her room before anybody saw the tears streaming down her face. "Why did I do that?" she asked Sarah, who was wide-awake and staring up at her. "Why did I let that happen when I knew it couldn't go anywhere?"

Sarah's answer was a little babbling that ended with *Mama* and *Daaa*…two words that weren't going to come together. Angela's answer, the one in her heart, was that she was falling in love with Mark. It wasn't a good enough answer, but it was the only one she had.

CHAPTER EIGHT

"Scotty? Are you awake?" Angela asked, hoping the boy would get up without a tussle. But he simply rolled over and ignored her. All the other children had been up an hour. They'd had breakfast, and were already on a nature hike, being led by Fallon, James and Tyler Galbraith. All, except Scotty, who was being cantankerous this morning. "It's time to get up, sleepyhead," she said, giving him a gentle nudge.

"No!" he barked, pulling the blankets up.

More than any other child at camp, he was the one who needed the exercise, as he was nearly twenty pounds over his ideal weight. But three days in, and she was discovering that Scotty and anything that involved physical activity didn't mix well. He was seven and, to all intents and purposes, sedentary. Video games, TV, snacks…his life. Which would turn into a very bleak future for him if they didn't get his situation straightened around, get him taught, get him motivated. "No isn't an option, Scotty. It's time for you to get up, get dressed, have breakfast—"

"*I said, no!*" He jerked away from Angela when she tried to pull the blanket down.

"He's not getting up?" Mark asked from the doorway. He was standing there holding Fred, who was decked in a little red plaid doggie jacket, looking quite stylish.

"I've tried everything except just pulling him out of bed,

and he's resisting it all." She looked at the boy, who'd balled himself into an almost fetal position, with his back to them. "Any suggestions?"

He grinned. "Maybe if I toss Fred in the sack with him, that will get a response."

"Do you like dogs, Scotty? Because we have a nice one here, who would like to be your friend."

"No," Scotty snapped.

Angela and Mark raised eyebrows at each other then Mark shook his head, almost apologetically. "Well, I'd like to hang around and figure this out, but Fred needs to go visit the great outdoors for his morning constitutional, and after that I have a couple of candidates to interview for the course." He walked over to the bed, gave Scotty a little jostle on the shoulder. "And you, young man, need to get up and moving. As soon as I'm done, I'm coming back, and you and I are going to take that hike together. It'll be good for both of us." He winked at Angela. "The longer you stay in bed, the longer the walk will be."

"Don't want to," Scott mumbled.

"His speech…" Angela said. "It's…it's slurred." Without another thought she grabbed hold of Scotty and tried rolling him over. He lashed out, started kicking and punching. She took a right cross to the eye, knew instantly she'd have a shiner soon.

Mark put the dog down and ran forward to help. "Angela, are you OK?"

She waved away his concern, focusing all her energies on helping Scott. "Don't worry, I'm fine. Can you get me a blood-sugar testing kit? I can manage Scotty."

Grabbing Fred, Mark raced from the room. "Scotty, calm down!" she told the boy. "We're trying to help you."

"Leave me alone!" he sobbed, trying to escape her arms. Her first thought was that he'd hurt himself, flailing the way he had. Her second thought was that something was going wrong. "Scotty, please... Calm down, sweetheart, it's OK. It's OK," she murmured gently over and over again as she sat down on the bed and held him firmly in her arms.

"Can you hold him still long enough for me to get his blood tested?" Mark asked, running back into the room. He had his medical bag with him, along with the blood-sugar testing kit.

"He's running out of energy. I'll keep him as still as I can."

Mark took hold of Scotty's hand and Scotty immediately yanked it back. The balance between needing to do the procedure and not hurting Scotty was precarious, but Mark took his hand again and successfully stilled him for a moment.

"No! I don't want that," Scotty screamed. "Leave me alone." He bucked up when Mark tried to prick his finger, caught Angela unawares, knocked her off the side of the bed. If it hadn't been for Mark standing directly behind her, bracing himself against her to add support, she would have been thrown to the floor.

"Get yourself into position to prick his finger," Mark said. "Because I can't do it from this angle."

"How about we trade places? You hold him, I'll get his blood." So Mark held Scotty, his voice gently reassuring the boy, while Angela did the deed, pressing the lancet to Scotty's index finger. After she pressed it, she squeezed out a drop of blood onto the test strip. It was an easy thing to do, really, but for her a monumental procedure. Handing off the strip to Mark, she made her way back onto the side of the bed, trying again to hold Scotty during his tantrum.

"Four hundred and twenty," Mark said.

Dear God, that was high! She knew the numbers, knew what they meant and, suddenly, she felt sick to her stomach. "Mark, how could that have happened to him?" One of the conditions of the camp was that the kids didn't get to have contraband food. Nothing from the outside. And since kids will be kids, it was established with the parents that frequent checks would be made of the lockers and beds. Yet somehow Scotty had managed to circumvent their efforts.

"Well, I think the bag of cookies under the blanket is probably a start." He held it up for her to see. Empty. Totally empty, without so much as a crumb left. "Who knows what else he's been sneaking?" He looked down at Scotty, who hadn't gone exactly limp but who wasn't fighting the fight any longer. "Scotty, what else?" he asked. "I need to know what else you were eating all night."

"Nothing," the boy insisted. "They're not mine."

"Look, son. We want to help you. I've got to give you medicine and it would be better if I know what you've eaten."

Scotty's eyes welled with tears and it seemed to Angela that he might have just made the connection with the way he was feeling to the foods he'd eaten. She hoped so, anyway.

"She made me eat them." He nodded toward Angela, who'd finally let go of the boy but hadn't left his bed, just in case. "She said it was OK."

Mark glanced at Angela then back at Scotty. "You're not in trouble. We're not going to punish you, but you have to be honest with us."

Scotty refused to say anything more. Big tears were rolling down his cheeks, and he was sniffling. His eyes were also fluttering shut, and not so focused when they were open. "We'll figure it out later, Scotty," she said, pulling the boy back into her arms. "First thing we need to do, though, is take care of you." Looking up at Mark, she said, "We'll be fine while you make whatever arrangements you have to make for his treatment."

"Actually, I don't want to leave him here. He's obviously got quite a tolerance for high blood sugar, but just in case something happens, I can't leave right now. What I need for you to do is go to the clinic, ask Walt for fast-acting insulin and tell him I need his help down here." They traded places, he on the bed, holding Scotty, she standing up.

"He's on the hike with the children and the Galbraith family."

"Then you'll have to get it." He told her the brand name, instructed her to get a syringe. "And the portable EKG machine. "I want to monitor him while I bring his blood sugar back down, and for a myriad of reasons, including cardiac complications, I don't want to bring it down too slowly. So I need to keep him monitored. But before you go, can you take his blood pressure for me?"

"Sure." The procedure was easy enough. While she'd never done it before, she'd seen it done dozens of times. So first she picked up the cuff.

"Wrap the cuff around his upper arm," Mark instructed, moving over a little to let her in as Scotty started to struggle again, though not as hard this time. "Shut off the valve, pump up the bulb."

"What do I listen for?" she asked.

"Put the bell of the stethoscope over the pulse point in his arm then pump up the cuff. When it meets with enough resistance that you can't pump it easily, open the valve just a little, then listen. You'll hear two distinct things. The first will be the beginning of his heartbeat. Note the number on the meter when you hear it. Then the next thing will be the end of the heartbeat. Note that number, too."

She understood what the numbers meant. Had studied that after she'd learned the word sphygmomanometer.

"Don't touch me!" Scotty cried as she tried slipping the cuff onto his arm.

"Whoa," Mark said, motioning for Angela to stop for a moment. "You've got to let her do this, Scotty."

"No, I don't!" he yelled. "It hurts!"

"A little bit. But I'll let you do it to me twice, if you hold still long enough to let me do it to you once."

Scotty didn't respond. He was beginning to fade out. So Angela stepped back up and took a second try at it, but the instant she got the cuff on the boy's arm, he revved up once more, but not with so much fight in him this time. "You promise?" he mumbled.

"I'll even let you listen to your heart," Mark said as Angela finally succeeded in getting the blood-pressure cuff pumped up. She listened. Listened….heard nothing for a moment, wondered if she'd failed. But then there it was. A distinct thudding. An amazing thing. "Systolic is…one fifty." She continued listening… "Diastolic is one hundred. Want me to take it again to make sure?"

Mark shook his head, smiled. "I trust you."

I trust you. Those words rang in her ears while she ran to the clinic to find the insulin and EKG machine, and she was still clinging to them when she came back to the room, only to find Mark sitting on the side of the bed, looking at a very listless little boy.

"What happened?" she asked.

"It's catching up with him. He's going lethargic."

"Not a coma?" she gasped.

"No. I think he just finally ran out of energy. Blood-sugar swings can really be exhausting. Our little fighter here has dozed off."

"Before or after he took your blood pressure?" She handed Mark the vial of insulin.

"Before, but I'll make good on my promise. Maybe even turn him into a junior doctor of sorts. Training him in a couple of procedures might make him think about his own situation." He held out the syringe to her. "Care to be the one?"

"I don't want to hurt him," she said, looking down at the syringe.

"What will hurt him is not giving him that insulin. Scotty's got needles in his future, probably for the rest of his life if he doesn't get himself under control. And if you're going to work around diabetic kids, you've got to learn to do this because there might not always be a doctor around when you need one. Saving a child's life could be up to you, and you alone, Angela. And after you've learned this end of a diabetic crisis, you're going to have to learn what to do on the other end when the blood sugar drops so low that a sugar snack won't get it back up fast enough."

"OK, then, where does he get it?" she asked, stepping up to the bed, feeling the full impact of Mark's words. He was right. She did have to learn. But he hadn't offered to teach her and she felt the sting of his rejection once more. Not good enough for his class, not good enough to teach. It hurt, but she bit back the emotion. This wasn't the time to get into it.

"Arm's as good a place as any. So is the belly or the thigh. Choose your site. And don't jab it deep. It's meant to be…"

"Subcutaneous," she said, trying to sound resolute even though she still felt stung. "A subcutaneous injection, also called sub-cu, is administered as a bolus into the subcutis, which is the layer of skin directly below the dermis and epidermis, collectively referred to as the cutis." She gave Scott the shot then stepped back. "And a bolus, by the way, is from the Latin for ball. It's the administration of a medication, with the purpose of raising its concentration in blood to an effective level. The administration can be given intravenously, by intramuscular or subcutaneous injection."

"Very good," he said, standing. "An admirable body of knowledge."

"Go ahead and say it," she snapped, finally not able to hold it in.

"What?"

"That it's an admirable body of knowledge for someone who doesn't know anything, as I don't…except for my little bits of book learning, which you probably think is silly. That's what you were thinking, wasn't it?"

Mark glanced down at the child, who was now fast asleep. "Look, I know we messed things up between us with that kiss, but we've got to work together."

"That kiss isn't what messed things up. Like you said, it was…nothing." A simple word that had stabbed her even more than she'd realized. "What's messed us up is *us*. I don't know why, don't care to spend time trying to figure it out. You'll be getting involved in your course soon, I've got my program to look after. And there really shouldn't be too many times in the future when our paths will cross. That's the way it is, and it's fine by me."

He didn't answer her right off. Not until he'd taken another blood-sugar reading. "Three-eighty."

She nodded, pleased he was doing better. "Does he need to go to the hospital?"

"Not now. If I can't get his blood sugar down sufficiently then, yes, we'll take him. But I want to watch him for a while because I think he's going to respond to treatment pretty well right here, and the hospital can be traumatic. I want to spare him that, if I can. So, what I'd like you to do is go get his mother down here. Someone's enabling this child, and she's likely to be the one. Now would be as good a time as any to have a serious talk with her, because he's too young to be going through this."

"You really think Helen gave him the cookies?" It wouldn't surprise her, but it did make her wonder why his mother would do that. Didn't she understand what could happen? Had she never seen the dire consequences of long-term, uncontrolled diabetes—complications heaped on other complications? It suddenly occurred to Angela that the parents needed a boot camp, too. Maybe a day or two tacked on when the parents came, stayed, took classes with their children. Or, at the end, maybe the children could teach a class to the parents. It was only a kernel of an idea, but she liked it, thought it worth developing. Actually felt excited about it. But felt overwhelmed by all the things that could go wrong.

Sighing heavily, she took the failure on herself. "I've got to do better."

"You?"

"Me. It's my responsibility. I brought the kids here, I promised to teach them, to look after them, and if something like this can happen…" She thought for a moment. "What if one of the other kids had gotten into his stash?"

"You can't predict these things, Angela. And you can't make them your fault. Bad things happen and they don't have to fall on your shoulders, even though you seem to think that's the way it has to turn out. Scotty got into some food he shouldn't have had, and you weren't the one standing there, handing it to him."

"Maybe I didn't give it to him, but I should have stopped it. Or found a way to keep this from happening."

He walked over to Angela, pulled her into his arms. "It's not about Brad telling you you're not good enough. It's about one little boy who found a way to cheat."

Resisting him, pulling completely away then stepping back to a respectable distance between them, she stiffened up. "This doesn't have anything to do with Brad."

"Doesn't it? Isn't he always in the back of your mind, telling you you're not good enough? No matter what the situation, doesn't he still control the way you act inside it?

Like now, when you're convincing yourself you're not good enough to run this program?"

"That's not fair!"

"It's not about what's fair, Angela. It's about what's happening to you. About your reality. About how you're still reacting to Brad, the b—" Mark looked down at Scotty, and even though the boy was sleeping, he mouthed the rest of the word.

This wasn't the time to argue about it. Mark was wrong. Or maybe he wasn't. She was confused. Angry at herself for not realizing what Scotty might do. Frightened for the boy. And...hurt. At times, Mark seemed to care about her and she felt so much better when he did. But at other times... "It's about Scotty," she said, trying to sound decisive, even though she really felt wobbly. "What do we do about Scotty? Send him home so he can't accidentally cause problems with another child? Keep him here, spend more time with him, try harder to teach him? I mean, right now I'm leaning toward sending him home. He matters so much to me, Mark, and I'll continue working with him, one on one, at the hospital clinic. But I'm scared to death that if we can't keep a close enough eye on him..."

"We can't turn him away, Angela. I think that would be the easiest thing to do, but good medicine isn't always about the easiest thing."

That offended her. Of course she knew that. The problem was, she had eleven other children here who could easily give in to Scotty's temptations if he offered them the very same thing that had made him sick. So what Mark had said about good medicine... "It's not turning him away," she argued. "It's coming up with an alternative that will work for him."

He held firm. "By turning him away. That's your alternative."

She was offended even more this time. "Don't you get

it? I want to help him, but I'm not sure this is the place. Not around the other children."

"It's the *only* place, Angela. It has to be because if it's not, Scotty could get lost. Think he's not worth the effort. He could feel the rejection in ways we can't even anticipate. Which means you have to make this camp the place, not just for him but for other kids just like him. Or kids who'll be here in the future who'll be even more inclined to be a problem. It's something we'll have to factor into the program and plan for because not all the kids are going to be easy and cooperative. And the worst of them are the ones who'll need this the most. Rejecting them…" He shook his head, closed his eyes, sighed heavily. "Telling them they're too bad to be here could only force them to do the things they need to be here to correct. It's a shaky emotional balance."

What she saw on his face, heard in his voice…it wasn't a side of Mark she'd seen before. He cared. Cared deeply. And he still wanted to walk away from it? She didn't understand that, didn't understand it at all. But he was right about everything, and the perspective he'd just put in front of her scared her because she knew what it was like to live with shaky emotional balance. She'd spent what had seemed like a lifetime there. So she had to trust Mark in this. Trust his deep insight into kids, like Scotty, who would take more effort. It was a shame, and a terrible waste that medicine was soon going to lose Mark, though, because he had so much to give. Maybe he just didn't know how much. Maybe, in time, he'd find himself again. "OK, I'll admit it. You've made your point. I've got to get myself prepared to deal with kids like Scotty. And *not* send them away. That was me in panic mode, I think. I'm nervous about the program, Mark, and I don't feel especially suitable to run it. I mean, what in my life has prepared me for this?"

"Everything you've done, everything you are. Neil and

Eric wouldn't have approved you if they hadn't believed you were the one. As much as they like you personally, they wouldn't have offered you this opportunity if they hadn't trusted you with these kids. The thing is, you've got to quit letting your ex-husband get to you. He's a loser. An idiot for walking away from you and Sarah. And that's got to become your mantra. *He's an idiot...he's an idiot.*"

Angela laughed. "Do you know how nice it is to hear someone say out loud what I've been thinking all this time?"

"Doctor's prescription—say it loud once every hour and soon you'll start believing it."

She watched him walk over and take Scotty's pulse, then check his blood pressure. She was the one who did a finger stick on the boy for his blood-sugar reading. "Two-eighty," she said, in obvious relief. "It's amazing how fast he's responding."

"We work well together," he said, almost offhandedly. Then he squeezed her shoulder, let his hand linger a moment longer than it should have, then slid it down her arm when he removed it.

They did work well together. Which made her feel sad for the opportunity she wouldn't have learning from him, because Mark Anderson was a good teacher. More than that, he was a good doctor and a good person. And temporary. She had to remember that. At moments like these, when her pulse was galloping thanks to one little touch, she had to remind herself that he was leaving and she was staying.

"And about that kiss…"

Her breath caught in her throat. "I think you said everything you wanted to say about it."

"I need to apologize. Afterwards, what I said…"

"That it was a mistake?"

"It was, but not in the way I think you took it. What I meant to say was that it was nice, but that we shouldn't be getting involved on that level. You have your plans, I have mine, and neither of us should put ourselves in a position that what we want could be jeopardized."

"You think that one kiss would jeopardize our future plans?" Now, rather than being offended, she was almost flattered.

"I said the wrong thing again, didn't I?"

"The kiss wasn't a mistake, Mark. Maybe to you it was, but it wasn't to me. It was nice, we let ourselves get carried away... I'll admit that when you said it was nothing I felt a little hurt. But I didn't dwell on it." Such a lie. She'd dwelt on it to the point of emotional weariness.

"You didn't? I did. More than I should have, or wanted to. Dwelt on the kiss, my reaction to it... You tempt me, Angela, and if I were in a place right now where I could give in to temptation..." He stepped closer to her. Ran a gentle thumb over her swelling eye. "You need some ice," he said. "And you need to quit being so hard on yourself. The people here in White Elk, the children in your program...they need you. Need all of you, including those pieces your ex-husband is still taking away." He nodded toward Scotty. "He needs you, too, in ways you probably can't even understand yet."

Everybody needed her but Mark. She knew he didn't, but it was nice fantasizing, for a moment, that he'd told her he was the one who needed her most. Those would have been wonderful words to hear. But she'd never hear them. She knew that. Had to face facts and move on. "I understand that," she said, her voice barely above a whisper as she looked over at the child lying in bed, his face angelic, like he hadn't a care in the world. The truth was, he had so many cares... dire ones, like she did. "OK, we start a new program just for Scotty. It's called being on watch, twenty-four-seven."

"I'll start by checking his room, look for his hiding places, several times a day." He grinned. "And every time he turns around, I'll be standing there with a lancet, ready to do a test if I think he's been cheating. He's a smart kid. He'll catch on pretty fast. And something we do here will save his life, Angela. That's what it's about. Saving his life."

Those were the words she couldn't ignore. *Save his life.* That's all she wanted to do for any of the children. Save their lives by teaching them how to take responsibility for themselves, for their condition. "I'll go and talk to Scotty's mother. I'll be the one to tell her what he's done and how we're going to deal with it. You can have her when I'm finished, and tell her the dire medical consequences if we don't get her son under control. Paint a grim picture, Mark. She needs to hear it. And in the meantime, I'm going to start putting together a plan for more parental participation in the camp. Maybe even some classes at the hospital for significant others only."

"You did a good job here, Angela. Your responses are quick, your instincts perfect."

"But it's not enough," she said wistfully.

"Not right now. But soon…" He kissed her gently on the forehead. "Now, I'm going to sit here with Scotty for a while. He'll sleep, but I want to wake him up shortly and make sure he's good. I'd suggest you go ice your eye, maybe take Fred for a quick walk for me, then see if you've got any foundation to cover Scotty's handiwork, because this time tomorrow it's going to be purple."

She laughed. "A badge of honor. I lost that battle, but I'm not about to lose the war." She bent over Scotty, pulled the blanket to his shoulders, brushed back a tuft of brown hair from his forehead. "You hear that, Scotty? I'm not going to lose this war."

Outside Scotty's room, standing in the hall, Angela watched Mark settle into a chair next to the boy. Mark, himself, was a war. The only thing was, she wasn't sure how she felt about him. They were certainly getting closer and under other circumstances she would define that closeness as something more than a growing friendship. But under *these* circumstances? He was leaving after all. It was inevitable. So, if things between them were to somehow develop even more in the next months, would she consider going with him, if he asked? The answer was simple, and it hit her fast. *Not with a man who didn't want her as much as she wanted him.* However, the real question was, did she truly want Mark? And if so, how much?

"Eventually, I'd like to be set up for ski lessons, but for this week sledding is the easiest way to go." Twelve children, twice as many adults, all with sleds, all over the place. The program was growing. Just a few days into it and people were dropping by, looking for ways to help.

"I never expected the magnitude of this," Mark commented. He was holding a round purple sled under his arm, ready to have his own go at the hill.

"That's the way it is, here in White Elk. People just want to help. It's why I stayed. When I came here it was to take a job. I like the alpine atmosphere, didn't want to spend the rest of my life running all over the world chasing the ski circuit, so when I saw that Pine Lodge had an opening for executive chef, I applied. Then fell in love with everything about White Elk, almost at first sight."

"And you'd never leave?"

She shook her head. "Sarah needs to be raised in a place like this. It's tough enough out there in the world. I've been there, done most of it, and I know how hard it is to get along. But when you're lucky enough to find a place that's…that's like family, why would you want to leave?" She looked up at him. "And I mean that literally, Mark. Why do you want to leave? You've been here since just before Christmas, and you're probably more a part of the community here than you've ever been anywhere else. You fit in, and people like you. They respond to you."

"But I'm still the same old person I always was. A doctor. Someone other people count on. And my whole point of leaving California was to not be me."

"There's nothing wrong with being you, Mark."

"There's everything wrong with being me." He visored his eyes with his hand, looked out over the hill. Drew in a deep breath. "Did you have that talk with Scotty's mother?"

Changing the subject didn't change the issues. But she wasn't going to get into that with him right now. The snow was good, she was in the mood to sled. "She's the one who gave him the food. Said she told him only to eat a little at a time, as a treat. That he knew he shouldn't eat as much as he did."

"She doesn't get it, does she?"

"A little bit of you rubbed off on me, Mark."

"Meaning?"

"I put on one of your scowls, told her that one of these days, when Scotty overindulges, someone might not be there to find him the way we did. That he could die if that happens. I also told her that I can't have him putting my other children at risk, and I think that was something she'd never considered."

"Do you think she'll do what she needs to?"

"I hope so. There was a lot of denial. But that's so often the case with those closest to the children. They want them to live a normal life like the other kids do, and somehow food gets all mixed up in that. Walt's going to give them an eye-opener tomorrow—the dire consequences of diabetes out of control. It's brutal, but they've got to know what they're dealing with, and I've invited all the parents to that lecture, too. They need it as much as their children do."

"Well, I'm going to have a little chat with Scotty in a few

minutes. He's the one, by the way, who's not playing, like the rest of the children are doing."

Angela looked over at the boy, who was sitting sullenly on a bench. "He won't exercise," she said. "He sits out every single time. Refuses. Tells me I can't make him do it."

"He's seven, and sedentary. And to be honest, I'm worried about him because his blood-sugar averages are too high, his blood pressure is elevated and all that is wreaking havoc with his body."

"Which is why I assigned him to you." she said, smiling. "Now, if you'll excuse me…" She took her own sled to the hill, laid down on it and rode the bumps all the way to the bottom. When she came to an inauspicious stop in a pile of snow, pretty much flat on her back, she looked back up to see if Mark was following her down. But he wasn't in sight. Not at the top, not at the bottom.

He'd gone to get Scotty. Maybe to have that chat, maybe to convince Scotty to sail down the hill just once. Whatever it was, he'd gone to get Scotty, and that was a good thing. Because the boy needed him. And Mark needed Scotty. "You'll find yourself," she whispered. Truly, he really wasn't as far away as he thought. Maybe buried at the moment, but not really lost.

"What are you doing with Sarah?" Angela asked. "Edith took the morning off to spend time with Fallon Galbraith, and Emoline was sitting with Sarah a little while ago."

"Emoline was called to the hospital, and there was no one else available but me." Mark shifted position, looking like a natural with a baby on his hip. Actually, he'd encouraged Emoline to go, promised her that he didn't mind babysitting for a while. And he didn't. Something about Sarah relaxed him, made him think about all those things he'd planned on for his own life so long ago, things that had made him happy for a little while, things that had *all* been a lie.

"You don't have a class right now?"

"Walt and I traded. He wants a little time alone with Catie later on, and as I didn't have any plans, I was glad to make the switch. Which worked out well because Sarah needed a play date now. And Sarah, Fred and I have been having a nice time, haven't we?" He asked that last of Sarah.

"I'll admit she looks happy."

"She's decided she loves sledding."

"You took my daughter sledding?"

Mark laughed. "Let's just call it a variation on a theme. But Sarah definitely has a preference for the great outdoors. We built a snowman, took a walk up to Hornaday Bluff..."

"No rock-climbing and skiing?" Angela asked, taking a very reluctant little girl back from Mark. So reluctant, in fact, that Sarah made her preference clear, holding onto Mark for dear life.

"I think she's expressing an opinion," he said over top of what was turning into some loud vocal protests. "Reminds me of you in a lot of ways."

"Sarah, it's OK," Angela said, trying to calm down her screaming daughter. But Sarah wasn't about to be consoled, not in Angela's arms at the moment.

"Want me to take her back?" Mark asked.

"Did you hypnotize her?"

He chuckled. "I'd prefer to think that it's just about my nice way with the ladies." He held out his arms for Sarah, and the child practically leapt over to him. And was immediately happy again.

"Look, if you have plans..."

"I did promise Sarah I'd teach her how to make a snowball." He tweaked Sarah's nose and her response to was to reach out and tweak him back. Something he'd worked on for the better part of an hour with her. Just to impress Angela.

"Did she just…? Mark? What's going on between you two, really?"

"We're getting along," he said, gesturing for Angela to follow him to the lodge's front door. "Sarah's teaching me what a one-year-old likes to do…"

"She doesn't talk."

"No, but she's got definite opinions. Just like her mother does." He pushed the door open and Angela preceded him outside. "What about her father?" he asked, once they were out on the front lawn.

"He's never met her. Doesn't want to be tied down to anything so permanent. He'd wanted me to…" She shook her head. "Let's just say that the pregnancy wasn't anything he wanted to invest himself in, and if I'd made other choices, he might have stayed for a while. At least, that's what he said at the time. His family loves Sarah, though. They've been great to her…great to me. But he hasn't even wanted to see a picture."

"It's amazing, isn't it? He's the luckiest man in the world, being father to this little spitfire, and he's too stupid to know it. And *stupid* is a mild word for what I'm thinking!" At the clearing near the front of the entryway fountain, he sat Sarah down on an ornamental rock, where three copper frogs, frolicking on the edge of the fountain, caught her attention.

"She doesn't need him, and I'm glad he's not part of our lives. I only want good things and good people around her. And he's not good. At least, not for my daughter."

"But what if he comes back someday? Changes his mind, decides he wants the daddy experience?"

"He lost that privilege when he asked me to have an abortion. As far as I'm concerned, he doesn't get it back. Besides, he doesn't want it. He's made that pretty clear in any number of ways. She's mine, not his."

"Stupid, like I said."

"I guess I have to agree with that. But what does that make me, hanging onto him for so many years?"

"Strong. Naive. Misguided, maybe. Not stupid, though."

"But I feel stupid now that I can finally see how he is."

"He's like my ex-wife. A mistake."

"A *stupid* mistake," she said, arching amused eyebrows.

"Different kind of stupid altogether."

Angela sighed. "What we do for love."

"In my case, not love. More like a delusional event."

"You mean a stupid event?" she asked, grinning.

"OK, stupid. But I got over it."

"So did I. And the good thing is I got Sarah. That makes up for everything."

"It sure does." Mark bent down, scooped up a little handful of snow. "Now, Sarah, the object here is to make it nice and round." He dropped to one knee in front of her and showed her the steps to rounding out a nice, perfect snowball, even though she was still more interested in the copper frogs. "The reason you want it to be round is so that when you throw it at your mommy, it will travel far enough to hit her."

Angela laughed. "You want her to hit me?"

"In years to come, when she's a teenager, and you're tearing out your hair over something's she's done, you'll long for the days when it was only about a snowball."

"Daaa…" Sarah responded.

"That's right," Angela said. "You can hit Daaa with a snowball, too."

"Not what I had in mind," Mark said, placing the snowball in Sarah's tiny hand. "Now, what you need to do is rear back just a little before you throw…" He kept her hand in his for a moment, then moved it enough that the snowball flew out and landed on his knee.

"Good job!" Angela said, bending to give her daughter a kiss. "Very good job, Sarah. I couldn't have aimed better myself."

"You want to hit me with a snowball?" Mark asked.

"No. Not as long as I have Sarah to do my dirty work." Angela scooped up another little handful of snow, rounded it into a ball then handed it to Sarah, who immediately threw it down on her own. "She's a natural," Angela boasted, turning to Mark.

His reply was a soft snowball right smack in Angela's face. Which made Sarah laugh with delight.

"You know this is war, don't you?" Angela said, scooping up more snow, rounding it and launching it at Mark, hitting him in the shoulder.

His reaction was to hide behind Sarah. "It's just you and me, kid," he said to her.

"Hiding behind the baby now, are you?" Angela said, threatening him with a snowball half the size of his head. "Step out from behind the child and I'll go easy on you."

"Should I believe her, Sarah?" he asked, placing a baby-sized snowball in her hand. But this time he didn't let go of her hand, he guided it into a launch of the snowball and, amazingly, it launched a good two feet, before dropping and hitting Angela on top of her snow boot.

Angela's response was to scoop that snowball up and as-similate it into her own. "Coward," she accused, arching her eyebrows and keeping a poker face underneath them.

Damn, she was sexy. Even playing in the snow, she had such an effect on him. "I'm just staying loyal to the fairy prin-cess here. Protecting her from the likes of the evil snowball queen."

"But the evil snowball queen only has eyes for you." She

showed him the giant snowball in her hand. "And it has *your* name on it. So step out here. Take it like a man."

"Should I surrender?" he whispered to Sarah.

Her response was to stretch out her hand and wiggle her fingers. Well, the assumption was a wiggle since her snowball fight was taking place in mittens.

"You saw her answer. She's in this to the end. She wants a snowball...*your* snowball."

"That's what she said?" Angela laughed.

"As plain as the red nose on your face. The fairy princess has claimed her victory and the evil snowball queen must surrender her snowball. I'm sorry, but the decision is final."

Angela knelt down to her daughter. "Then I surrender." She laid her giant snowball down and bent to kiss Sarah's chubby cheek. When she did so, Mark seized the opportunity, grabbed up the snowball, and...

"No," Angela squealed, falling backwards.

That's when Mark pounced right on top of her, his knees straddling her, his snowball poised right above her face. "It was *her* idea," he said, nodding sideways at Sarah. "I'm just the minion here."

"You wouldn't," Angela said, looking him straight in the eye.

"If it were up to me, I probably wouldn't. But the choice clearly isn't mine. So, Sarah..." He turned to look at her. "What will it be? The snowball, or not?"

"Daaa..."

"You heard her. It was her decision, not mine." Mark pushed the snowball straight down into Angela's face, and didn't try one iota to resist her when she came back up at him, fighting. In fact, he rather enjoyed the fight as she struggled to flip over and pin him down. The skirmish lasted all of thirty seconds then when she was on top and he was the one flat in the snow, he looked up and smiled. "I win."

"But I'm on top," she protested.

He winked at her. "I know you are. Which is why I win."

She bent down, dangerously close to his lips, then whispered, "You're bad, Dr. Anderson," then proceeded to smush a snowball in his face. "Good plan, Sarah," she said rolling off Mark and grabbing Sarah into her arms. "He never saw it coming."

The truth was, he had. But nothing in him had wanted to stop it. Lying here in the snow with Angela and Sarah, the three of them probably looking like idiots to passersby, this was the only place he wanted to be right now. *The only place.*

CHAPTER NINE

"Sound asleep. Even before I got her into bed." She crept out of the suite's bedroom and closed the door quietly behind her, taking one last look back at Sarah before she did so.

Mark was seated on the sofa, with Fred asleep in his lap, snoring gently. "She has a lot of energy. I wouldn't have expected her to stay up and be so alert for as long as she did."

Angela dropped down beside him, stretched out, relaxed. Appreciated the nice, cozy feeling. A feeling she didn't have too often. "She was enjoying herself. And the one thing I'm going to make sure Sarah learns is that she has to enjoy her life. When something amazing comes around, grab it and hang on. There are so many other serious things happening, situations that will pull us down if we let them, and it's those moments of pure pleasure that will make the difference, make life bearable. Kind of like a beacon, I suppose. Something you know is there, something shining out in the dark, waiting for you to latch onto it. She has to know that beacon is there for her."

"But you don't take that advice yourself. Someday, when she's older, won't she notice that? Won't she realize that while you're teaching her one thing, you're doing something entirely different? Will she see any enjoyment, or fulfillment, in you, Angela? Will she see you reaching out for that beacon yourself, or turning your back on it because you have yet another goal to accomplish?"

"That's not fair. My goals will ensure that Sarah does have those beacons in her life. But I do have fun, and I'm certainly fulfilled. I spend time with Dinah and her family, I cook. I deal with these amazing kids on a daily basis now, here and at the hospital. And I have Sarah. It might not be anything you'd enjoy, anything that would fulfill you, but from where I'm watching it all happen, it's all good." She paused for a moment. Closed her eyes, pictured all the good things in her life. Amazingly, Mark was one of them now.

"Fulfillment may be the simple things like snowball fights, especially if you're getting it with the people you care about. Or something on a much grander scale, like seeing your dreams for your daughter coming true. But if you limit your fulfillment to only isolated incidents, to things that may happen on rare occasions, you're missing out on all the other amazing things around every minute of every day And I don't want Sarah missing out on any of that. I want her to see everything, to experience everything. And not with a narrow view the way I did for most of my life. The way *you* do now. I want so much more for her than that, Mark." With a weary sigh, she kicked off her shoes and pulled her feet up.

"You think my view is narrow?"

She twisted to look at him. "Isn't it? You're here to teach one thing, then you're leaving, when there could be so many good things here for you, things that, if you'd let them, would be your reason to stay. But leaving is all you see in front of you, which, in my opinion, makes your focus about as narrow a one as I've ever seen."

"Earlier, I taught a class on ocular health and how it relates to the diabetic condition. Then I taught a class what the hemoglobin A1C means in terms of their overall health.

I taught that class, by the way, in the snow, using the various components of a snowman as my example. You know, the more out of balance the various parts are, the more unstable the snowman. So how do you figure that's narrow?"

"It's narrow because Neil and Eric are appealing to your greater sense of obligation to be here and do all this. It's not you being here on your own, doing it on your own. And there's a difference."

"Not really. They're trying to put all my little pieces back together again because they're good friends. You know, trying to fix a broken friend, while I'm trying to help out some friends who need help. It's not a big deal."

"Because you want to be *fixed*?"

"Because I'm not as narrow as you think." His voice gentled. "Neil Ranard and Eric Ramsey are the two best friends I've ever had, and I wouldn't have turned them down, no matter what the circumstances. In my own life, I may be pretty far gone. But you don't turn your back on friends."

"You're not as *gone* as you let on."

"What I'm not is in anything for the long haul. If you want to call that a narrow view, feel free. I call it a goal, not unlike the goals you have. Except mine are simple. Get it done, get out. No lists."

"And my goals are moving me toward something, while yours are moving you away."

"You're right. I'll admit it. Mine are moving me away from…everything I want to move away from. Your goals are admirable, mine are survival. Self-indulgent, some people would call it." He sat Fred down onto the sofa next to him and reached over, picked up Angela's feet, pulling her into a foot-rub position.

"You may be a lot of things, Mark Anderson, but you're not self-indulgent." She settled back into the cushions to enjoy the feel of his hands on her feet. Now, if anything could ever be called self-indulgent, this was it. She liked being pampered. Wasn't used to it, but she definitely could get used to it. Especially from Mark. "You really don't have to do this," she said, hoping against hope he wouldn't quit.

"If I had the narrow view you seem to think I have, I'd probably agree. But my view is wide enough to see how you're running about twenty-five miles a day, between the camp and your daughter. And I have it on good authority that you're still managing hospital dietary stuff from here. So, in my not-so-narrow view, I think that deserves a foot rub."

His first squeeze to the arch of her left foot was pure heaven, and all she could manage in reply was a contented sigh.

"Not bad for a man with a narrow view?"

"Maybe I'm changing my mind, because I've never had a foot rub before, and this is so—"

"Did he ever treat you nicely?" Mark interrupted. "Indulge you a little bit? I mean, I was the first with flowers, but I can't believe I'm the first with a foot rub."

The question jolted her out of her languid mood. "What?"

"Treat you nicely. Did your ex-husband ever treat you nicely?"

She thought about it for a minute. Flashed back to those years, when she'd been the one doing the pampering, doing the indulging. The one giving *all* the foot rubs, *all* the back rubs… "Probably not. But at the time I don't suppose I realized that."

"But he never hurt you."

She shook her head. "Not physically. Brad's not a violent type. Not even a mean type. I don't think he ever sets out to intentionally hurt anybody. But the thing is, he never really considers anyone's feelings other than his own. So I guess you could call him selfish."

"And you never saw that in him?"

"Oh, I probably did. But I was deluding myself into thinking I could change him, that once I'd shown him how nice life could be after we'd settled down, he'd be happy to change. But the thing I never took into account was that we didn't want the same lives."

"You're not mad as hell at him over Sarah? For not being involved with her, not even wanting to see her?"

"Maybe I should be, but I'm not. It's his loss, not having her in his life. If anything, I should probably be sad for him because he's missing so many wonderful things. In all honesty, though, Brad wouldn't be a good father. A child requires so much attention and Brad wouldn't know how to handle himself if someone around him needed more attention than he did. Too bad, too, because Sarah's the best thing he'll never get to know."

"You're an amazing woman, Angela Blanchard. Because I'm still mad as hell at my ex-wife, and there's nothing in me that wants to change the way I feel."

Angela sat up a little bit, to look at him. Not enough, though, to pull her feet out of his amazing touch. "Hanging onto the anger will tie you in knots. As long as you're dealing with it you can't move on."

"But what if I want to stay angry? What if she deserves that anger every day I can give it to her?"

"She might deserve it, Mark, but do you? Because the anger will cost you, not her. She's not here, she's not seeing it or feeling it. Which means the anger is for you. Not her."

He squeezed her arch too hard and she flinched.

"Is it because your father-in-law died? Is that why you're so angry at yourself? Because, as a doctor, you know that sometimes the hard choices don't work out the way you want them to. I've seen that with Eric. Two months ago he lost a patient—a little girl. She had leukemia, and he'd done everything in his power to make her better. Dinah said he didn't sleep, didn't eat… And after she died he sat in a dark room for two days, refusing to let anybody in. He hated losing that child, but he dealt with it because that's what you deal with when you're the doctor. And I know you've gone through losing other patients…"

"Not the same."

"No, it's not the same. And I can't even begin to imagine what it's like when that patient is someone you love. But you yourself said he wanted you to take care of your wife first. How could you *not* do that?"

"The thing is, I think he probably knew he was dying, but he also knew that…that my wife was pregnant."

"What?"

"Not far along. Not far enough for her to tell me. But her father knew. And naturally he wanted her cared for first."

"I do understand that. If it were between Sarah and me…" She shook her head, trying to rid herself of the sad picture there. "It would always…*will* always…be Sarah." Once again, the pressure he applied to her foot turned hard, almost to the point it hurt. So she wiggled out of his grasp and sat up, cross-legged, looking at him. "You can't fault the man for that, or even be angry with yourself for how it turned out. You weren't the one making the choice."

"No, I wasn't. But I'm mad as hell anyway for the way it turned out."

"The baby. Did your wife…?"

He shook his head. "At the hospital, the doctor told me how lucky she was. She had some substantial cuts on her face, some that would require plastic surgery. *After* she had the baby. That's how I found out." He frowned the frown she knew so well. "After that, I had a month to live with that pregnancy, trying to console my wife over the death of her father, trying to keep her calm for the baby's sake. Trying to remember that Tom had given his life to protect that baby. And in that month I became quite the doting husband. Started making plans, thinking about what it was going to be like being a father. Of course, I was blocking out the fact that my wife was in a different place altogether. Fixing on her scars. Obsessed with not looking pretty. And hating me, at the same time, because her dad was dead. The accident was my fault, not saving his life was my fault. Her scars…"

"Your fault."

He nodded. "But that was fine, because if she needed someone to blame, which she did, I had broad shoulders. And all along I was sure it would get better once the baby was born. Honestly, I didn't give the marriage a chance, but at that point it was all about…" He swallowed hard. Didn't finish the sentence. "Then one day Norah went on a trip. Didn't tell me, didn't let me know where she was. I was worried to death. Hired an investigator to look for her. No luck. But two months later she came home without facial scars and also without our baby. She'd had an abortion because the plastic surgeon wouldn't do elective surgery on her while she was pregnant."

"I can't… I don't know what to say."

"*She* did. She told me the only reason she'd wanted the baby, to make her father happy. He'd wanted a grandchild. With Daddy gone, there was no reason to continue the pregnancy. So she didn't."

"Without telling you? Didn't you even have a clue?"

"You'd think I should have, wouldn't you? But no. Once again, I'd missed the obvious. So what the hell kind of a track record is that for a trauma surgeon?" He shut his eyes. "And you can't get around the fact that I should have seen it coming."

"But even if you'd known, could you have stopped her?"

"I've asked myself the same question a million times. Maybe I could have said something…convinced her to wait a few more months. Hell, I'd have gotten on my knees and begged if it would have done any good. But…"

"But she did what she wanted to do. And it wasn't your fault, Mark. She made a horrible, regrettable decision that was *not* your fault."

Mark dropped his head back to the sofa. Opened his eyes, stared up at the ceiling. "And you wonder why I'm leaving medicine? Well, that's it. The most important thing in my life that I should have seen coming, and I missed it. Totally missed it."

"Because that's what Norah intended. She hid it from you. And, as you recall, I already *did* trust my daughter to you. Remember? After you pulled us out of the Christmas train, when the avalanche covered us…you were so good with Sarah. And with her hysterical mother. I trusted her with you then, and I would right now."

"Then you'd be wrong to do it."

"I burnt a perfectly good goulash last month. Maybe the best goulash I've ever made."

He twisted his head to look at her. "What?"

"Goulash. You know, stew beef, tomatoes, onion, garlic, paprika…Hungarian goulash. It was cooking away ever so nicely, then all of a sudden it was burnt to a crisp. Smoking in the pot."

"OK, so you burnt your goulash. And that means…?"

"In and of itself, nothing. Goulash is easy to burn. But the thing is, I know that's the case when I cook it. Most of the time my goulash makes it to the table, gets served up on some rather tasty homemade poppy-seed noodles, instead of being dumped down the drain. Yet that wasn't the first pot of goulash I've lost."

"Are you comparing your situation to mine? You lost goulash, I lost…"

"Not at all. What I'm talking about are the expectations we set ourselves. I fully trust that my next goulash will be perfect. Why do I believe that? Because I know I can do it. I've had setbacks, but I've had successes, and every time I set out to make a goulash, I intend it to be a success, know that I can do it. Or else why bother? But you've lost what you intend for yourself, what you know you can do. All you can see are the setbacks now, and you've lost sight of the successes. You had horrible setbacks. Two of them, actually. Something I'm *not* comparing to burnt goulash, by the way. And you're not letting yourself get past all that because it's easier to stay where you are, being angry at yourself for what you didn't see or do or couldn't anticipate, rather than moving forward with the belief or trust that comes of knowing what you can do. I know I can make a good goulash, but what do you know, Mark?"

"And what's that supposed to mean?" He stiffened in defense. "What the *hell* is that supposed to mean, Angela?"

"See, right away you're challenging me, when you should have said you *know* you're a good doctor. Deep down, I believe you do know that, but somehow that got buried so deeply you can't find it right now, so you're running away from the things that remind you of what you think you've lost. And if you let yourself back into that place in your life where you truly take that knowledge to heart, to where you allow yourself to fully trust that you're still that good doctor, in spite of the setbacks, you run the risk of hurting yourself again, or admitting that you have human frailty like the rest of us do. You've put yourself so high up on a pedestal, Mark, that even *you* can't see yourself, and your expectation is that's where you should be, no matter what. Facing the fact that the pedestal gave way has become your biggest obstacle. It's what you're running away from…running away from the fact that you're just like the rest of us.

"But you know what? You're not the gruff doctor who goes around scowling all the time. That's a facade. The one meant to keep people way, the one meant to keep people from seeing that you're scared to death of being up there so high. You're the doctor who takes everything to heart too much, and it hurts you, and you don't want people to know that, don't want them to see that you're struggling to get through the best way you can. And I don't know why that is. Don't know why you've got all these unrealistic expectations of yourself."

He shoved up off the sofa, his face red with anger. "You know what? I have a new goal for your list, *Counselor*. You think you've got an answer for everything, so why not turn that into your next conquest? I hide behind unrealistic expectations for myself, and you hide behind too many expectations. I don't want to accomplish enough and you want to accomplish too much. So maybe I am running. I'll admit that. But aren't you running as hard and fast as I am? Just in a different way?"

His raised voice startled Sarah, who woke up with a cry. Angela was immediately off the couch, running to get to her daughter. No time to make it right with Mark now. No time for anything. Not now, and not when she returned to the main room of the suite moments later, with Sarah bundled in her arms, sniffling. Mark was gone by then. Gone, along with Fred. Out the door without so much as a slam. But she felt the slam. In her heart. "So, Sarah," she said, taking her daughter to the tiny kitchen area for a snack. "This is where I tell you that we're fine, just the two of us. That we don't need anybody else in our lives. Especially not—"

"Daaa…" Sarah said, looking out over the empty room.

"You're right. Especially not Daaa." The thing was,

though, she did want him in her life. "And he does give the best foot rubs." More than the foot rubs, though, she simply liked having him there. Liked it more and more each day. But she'd already wasted so many years chasing one man all over the world, and every road she'd taken, except the one that had gotten her to Sarah, had turned into a dead end. All Mark was showing her, so far, was a dead end. So, could she do that again? Could she chase after another man who was determined *not* to settle down?

One look at Sarah was all she needed. "Foot rubs or not, we don't need him. Even if we do want him. And we do want him, don't we, Sarah?"

The answer to that question didn't lie in her head. It rested in her heart, a heart that was on the edge of shattering. Because, no matter what she wanted, her choices were clear. And Mark couldn't be one of them.

"You're looking…tired." Dinah took Sarah from Angela, but rather than heading straight for the door she stayed standing in the doorway for a moment, watching her sister. "Something you care to talk about?"

Angela shook her head. "I didn't get much sleep last night, and I'm just tired."

"The kids keeping you awake?"

"The kids are fine. I think we exhausted them yesterday, with all the outside activities. And I think restructuring their diets is having some effect. Mellowing them out a bit."

"Scotty Baxter?"

"He's OK, so far. Trying harder to keep up with the other kids, which is good. We're keeping a closer eye on him, and Mark is working hard, trying to make him understand that just one candy bar can cause a whole series of unfortunate events. So far, it's working. Mark's got a good way with the children. They love him."

"So do you, don't you?"

Angela looked over at her sister. "Would it matter if I did?"

"Have you two talked?"

"I think we're past that now." She shook her head. "It ended before it even got started."

"Then he's not worth trying again?"

"I've got so much going on right now…"

"Which keeps you at your own distance. The more you do, the less you have to get involved on that level where you'd have to take a big risk? In other words, hiding behind your goals and ambitions? Line them up all around you so nothing can get in and hurt you again?"

Practically the same thing Mark had said to her. "That's not true! I'm totally involved here."

"But are you involved the way you want to be for the rest of your life? Because if you keep pushing people like Mark away from you, this *is* the rest of your life." Dinah hitched Sarah up on her hip and stepped into the hall. "Look, I don't want to keep lecturing you. You're doing good things with your program. You're a great mother. Eric is singing your praises as a dietician at the hospital. It's a good life, Angela. You've put Brad behind you, even if you don't know that yet. And I think when you finally come to terms with it, that's when you'll figure out the rest of your life. Anyway, the girls are planning a tea party for Sarah. They've invited friends, baked cookies, so stop by later if you have time. If not, I'll bring her back before bedtime."

Angela rushed forward to give Sarah a big hug. "You tell your Aunt Dinah that your mommy is just fine." She gave her daughter a kiss then looked up at her sister. "*Just fine.*"

"Just fine, and all alone." Dinah twisted her mouth into a half-smile then backed away. "If that's what you want, what you really want, I won't say another word about it. Except…"

She patted her flat belly. "Wouldn't you like to have another one of these some time?"

"What?"

Dinah arched her eyebrows, smiled fully. "You know what!"

It took a moment to sink in, but when it did Angela grabbed her sister into a hug so tight that Sarah protested. "When did you find out?"

"Did the home test this morning."

"And Eric?"

"Walking a couple feet off the ground. We're not telling the girls until much later, not really mentioning it to anyone outside immediate family because it's nice, having this feeling between the two of us, something special. Of course, I'm not telling you anything you don't already know. Except that you got cheated the first time, Angela, going through it with, or as it turned out without, Brad. Because doing this with Eric is like…" She smiled again. "I don't even know how to describe it. Except to say that I want this for you, too. You deserve it. You deserve to feel good for no other reason than some wonderful man adores you. And I think he does."

Angela laid her hand on her sister's belly. Kept it there for a moment. Felt the tears welling up in her eyes. "I'm happy for you. So happy…"

"I know you are. But I want you to be happy for you, too. Look, I'm late and I'm sure the twins are getting impatient." She leaned over, kissed her sister on the cheek. "High tea's at three. Stop by if you can."

Angela gave Sarah one more kiss then shooed the duo out the door. But when she shut the door behind them, everything felt so lonely, so empty. And it wasn't just the emptiness of the lodge suite bothering her. It was the emptiness inside her. Completely, totally inside her.

CHAPTER TEN

"Who's that?" Angela asked Emoline Putters. She was referring to the woman, who was pacing back and forth, like a nervous cat, through the lodge lobby.

"Her name's Karen Landry. She's asking for Dr. Anderson. More like demanding his presence."

"Did she say what for?"

Emoline shook her head. "Said she needs him right away. Won't talk to anybody else."

Angela chuckled. "The word is stat."

"I think the word is nuisance, but that's just my opinion. Anyway, his cell phone is off. I think he's in a session with one of the children right now, and I'm not inclined to interrupt him."

"Then don't. I'll take care of her myself."

"From the look of it, she's not going to be happy about that."

"What she's not going to be is standing in the lobby much longer. Until this lodge opens for business, this is a private venue and I don't want *any* unauthorized people here." Bracing for what she feared wasn't going to be pleasant, judging from the look on Karen Landry's face, Angela marched straight up to the woman. "May I help you?"

Karen reared back, like she was preparing to leap and fight. "I told that woman I need to see Dr. Anderson."

"Dr. Anderson isn't available. And he won't be for the rest of the morning."

"It's an emergency. He has to be the one. He'll understand."

Angela pulled her cell phone from her pocket and held it out to Karen. "If it's a medical emergency, call the hospital. Someone there will understand, too. The number is—"

"I can't!" she screamed. "Don't you people understand? I have a...a situation that needs Dr Anderson, and I demand to see him. Now!"

Two of the camp children strolling though the lobby stopped to listen, and Emoline moved them away.

"What's your situation?" Angela asked, not sure what to make of this. "Explain it to me, and I'll see what I can do to get Dr. Anderson down here."

Karen considered that option for a moment then gave in with an impatient huff. "It's Aimee. My daughter. I...I dropped her off here last night. Told her to come in and sit down in the lobby and when someone asked her what she was doing to tell them she was waiting for Dr. Anderson. That's all the child was supposed to do. Sit, wait and ask for Dr. Anderson."

Angela's stomach turned over. This wasn't making any sense. "Emoline," she called. "Get Mark." She took a deep breath. "Your little girl...what time did you drop her off?"

"Around seven. And like I said, she knew what she was supposed to do. Which is why I can't understand what happened."

Dear God, no one had reported seeing the child. "Let me get this straight. You left her here. And I'm assuming you didn't come back to get her, which is why you're here now?"

Karen shook her head. "I wasn't worried, because I knew she'd be safe here. Dr. Anderson told me this was a camp for children. But this morning, when no one had called me…" She frowned, shut her eyes for a moment, rubbed her forehead. "Did you lose her?"

"How old is your daughter?"

"Five."

"She's five and she's been missing since seven last night?" That was fourteen hours! "And you're only now starting to look for her?"

"Well, I don't know if it was that long. After all, she *was* here, in the lodge. Surely somebody would have looked after her. That's what you do here, isn't it? Look after children?"

"What's going on?" Mark demanded, running into the lobby.

"Dr. Anderson…" Karen started, practically falling into his arms. "My poor Aimee…*that* woman lost her." She glared at Angela.

He moved Karen back firmly. Looked at Angela. "What the hell is she talking about?"

"This woman claims she dropped Aimee off here last night to see you. And she hasn't heard from her since."

"You what?" The ice in his voice sent chills down Angela's spine.

Karen started to cry. "I knew you would call me to come get her. Or bring her home yourself. So I just thought…"

He turned his back on her. Focused on Angela. "Has anybody seen Aimee?"

"I'm making calls to everybody here," Emoline cried out over the commotion. "So far nobody remembers seeing her anywhere."

A lost child…five years old. It was all pounding in Angela's brain. "Are you sure she's here, Karen?" Angela managed to keep her voice calm. "Or are you making this up for attention?" She looked at Mark for clarification.

"I think she'd do it," he said.

"Do what?" Karen screeched. "Intentionally harm my daughter?"

Angela and Mark ignored the still crying woman. "We don't have enough people here to search the lodge, let alone start looking outside," Mark said, "and we can't leave the other children unattended while we look for Aimee."

Angela held up her cell phone, nodded. "Dinah," she said when her sister answered. "Tell Eric we have an emergency up at the lodge. We need all the search and rescue volunteers we can get. It's a missing child." No more was said. Angela clicked off. Swallowed hard. "So, in the meantime—"

"I'm going to start with the first floor," Mark said. He looked around. Shut his eyes for a moment. Turned in a slow circle.

Angela was fascinated by what she was watching. Didn't know what it was exactly. But Mark was in the moment, and she didn't want to interrupt whatever process he was going through. So she stayed back, held her breath, and observed, while Karen Landry sat in one of the chairs weeping and Emoline was on the phone, calling in every available volunteer she could think of.

"She wouldn't have gone beyond the first floor. Aimee's shy. Very small for her age. Not outgoing," Mark said. "She couldn't have used the stairs because I don't think she could have pushed the bar to open the stairwell doors unless she had help, or someone accidentally left one of the doors ajar. And I'm not sure she could have reached the elevator button without something like a pen or pencil. And she's not a devious little girl, so I don't think she would have thought of those things." He glared at Karen. "Unless instructed to."

She looked up at him, started to speak, but he waved her off with an angry flick of the wrist.

"Then we'll start down here. I'll take the west wing, you take the east," Angela said. "And when people start arriving, we'll have them spread out and search the other floors if we haven't found her by then." On her way past the front desk, she stopped next to Emoline. "Make sure every child is watched. This is going to disrupt everything, and I don't want them getting mixed up in it and wandering off or trying to join the search. When Eric gets here, call me. And…" She lowered her voice. "Go ahead and call the police. After we do find Aimee, we can't let her go home with her mother. The authorities are going to have to straighten this out."

Emoline nodded, sending a very wary glance in Karen's direction. "You just do what you need to do." She gave Angela's arm a squeeze. "I'll take care of things here."

"I don't divide my teams," Mark said, grabbing Angela by the arm. "In any rescue effort, we go in pairs. Safety in numbers, even when we're searching a lodge."

Angela didn't argue. She simply ran shoulder to shoulder alongside Mark to the farthest point in the east wing, which was still under construction and shut off by temporary construction doors. Locked. "She couldn't have gotten in there," Angela said, trying to open the doors, which wouldn't budge. She tried jiggling the padlock, but it was locked tight.

"Never underestimate the determination of a child who's either trying to hide or running away. I've found them hiding in places you'd never think to look, places that looked impossible to access. If Karen put her up to this, there's no telling where she could be, or how she got there."

"Do you think she did? I mean, do you think Karen actually came in here and hid her daughter somewhere? Or told her to hide?"

He stopped for a moment. "I'm not ruling it out. I see Aimee in the emergency room on a regular basis, and there's never anything wrong with her, yet Karen keeps bringing her back."

"Never anything wrong with her *yet*," Angela stated. "I've

read about Münchausen by proxy syndrome." Where a caregiver made up symptoms or even created medical symptoms in the person for whom they cared, in order to seek attention.

Mark arched his eyebrows in surprise. "Very good. Karen doesn't quite fit the profile, but she's very close… Unfortunately, ethically, there was nothing I could do except watch, and note the behavior." He fumbled with the key set until he found the master that let them through the construction doors then they stepped into the cavernous banquet room together. The room was chilly, several degrees cooler than the hallway outside. And even though sunlight was filtering in through the brown paper that was taped over all the windows while the walls were being painted, it was still dark. Eerie. Hollow.

"So, what happens to Aimee once we find her?" she whispered. "Because she can't go back to her mother now that she's done this."

"It doesn't always turn out that way," he warned her.

"You're talking about finding her?"

"We always go out expecting the best, but the reality is that sometimes the worst happens. And you've got to brace yourself for it, Angela."

"Can you ever get used to it?"

"No. And to be good in rescue, you shouldn't."

"Well, I'm only going to think the best. We're going to find Aimee, she's going to be fine, and we're going to ensure that she will be looked after properly in future."

He put his arm around her shoulder then pulled her into a hug. "I love your optimism," he whispered close to her ear. "And that's just the first thing on my list."

"You have a list?" she asked, reluctantly stepping out of his embrace.

"A very nice list that's growing all the time."

Her heart skipped a beat. "Will you ever let me see that list?"

"Maybe." He pulled his penlight from his pocket to take a good look around the room. Unfortunately, the small beam didn't give much light. "Aimee," he called, but not so loud it would frighten her. "It's Dr. Mark. Are you in here, Aimee?"

They checked the room, found nothing, and moved on through the back hall to the main kitchen area, where again they found nothing. On the way back down toward the main lobby, Emoline appeared with a very frightened Scotty Baxter in tow. "He wanted to talk to you," she said, then stepped away.

"Scotty?" Angela said, not sure what this was about.

"I can't find her," he said, on the verge of tears.

"Who?" Mark asked.

"That girl. The one everybody's looking for. I wanted to help find her, but she's not there now."

"Where?"

"Hiding behind the chair. That's where she was."

"When, Scotty?" Angela knelt down beside him. "Her name is Aimee. When did you see her?"

"Last night. She was hungry, and I gave her some…some cookies. But I didn't eat them. They were some my mom had in her office, but I only gave them to that girl. I didn't eat any. Then I went back to my room."

Angela made a mental note that while the lodge was a nice facility, it was too large. Too many places for the children to roam. They needed something more contained next time. *If* a next time happened. With one lost child in the balance, she wasn't sure about anything. "Did you see her after you gave her the cookies?"

He nodded. "When I looked out my window."

"This morning?"

"No. After I was suppose to be in bed. I was hungry, and I…" Tears slid down his cheek. "I didn't eat anything bad. Just my raw veggies, like you told me to."

Angela pulled him into her arms and hugged him. "You did a very good job, Scotty. I'm proud of you. So, do you know where she was going?"

"Home. She said she wanted to go home."

Angela looked up at Mark. "Where would that be?"

"I think Karen lives around on the back of the Middle Sister."

"Then let's hope the Indian lore holds true and the Three Sisters are protecting everybody within their shadows, because that's a long way, and I'm not sure a five-year-old would even know which direction to go." She looked at Scotty. "You've done a very brave thing here, trying to help us, Scotty. Did you happen to see which way she went?"

"To the back parking lot, I think."

"Good job. Now, we're going to take you back to the other children, and I want you to stay with them. Don't wander off again. Promise?"

His headed bobbed up and down, but he didn't speak. The thing about Scotty was that he lived in this lodge. This was his home. He knew it like none of the other children did, and if he said he'd seen Aimee heading to the back parking lot, she believed him.

Mark took Scotty by the hand and led him back to Emoline, while Angela took a call from Eric, who reported that he had thirty volunteers on his way up to the lodge and that Neil was prepping the mountain team to go out. She let him know that Aimee had, most likely, left the lodge last night. After she'd hung up, all she could think about was Aimee… Was she dressed warmly enough? Was she scared to death out there all by herself? Was she still alive? That was the thought she didn't want creeping in, but she couldn't keep it out. Reality check. She was beginning to see this situation the way Mark did, beginning to realize all the various options for outcomes, good and bad. Beginning, truly, to understand his world and how the tragedies could break his heart.

Impulsively, she called Dinah. She needed that connection with Sarah, even if only over the phone.

"She's right here in my lap," Dinah said.

"Can I talk to her?" Angela waited for a moment then said, "Mama loves you, Sarah." Feeling so much better knowing that Sarah was on the other end of the phone, and feeling sad that Mark didn't have that kind of an anchor in his life, she made an exaggerated kissing sound. "That's for your left cheek, and this one's for your right…"

On his way back through the hall, Mark heard the kissing sounds. Listened to Angela talk to her daughter. It was an amazing thing to behold. More than that, Angela was amazing. A woman who deserved…everything. For a moment he felt guilty about accusing her of hiding behind her ambitions. She wasn't hiding behind them. She was embracing them, living life to the fullest, taking everything she could take from it. While he was contented to…to what?

Actually, he wasn't sure, because nothing contented him anymore. Nothing, except being with Angela. Another thing on his growing list of things he loved about her—the way he felt when he was with her. "I think we need to move on. Gear up to go outside."

"I don't do that…the mountain rescue," she said. "I'm not part of the team, and I don't want to get in the way. For the first time, Mark, I really *do* understand."

"But I want you with me." He smiled, held out his hand to her.

"Are you sure?"

Mark pulled Angela roughly to his chest. "I didn't intend on meeting you in White Elk. Or anywhere else, for that matter. And it bothers the hell out of me that I did. But, yes, I do want you. So, ten minutes. We may be out there for a while, so dress appropriately."

He wanted her. The question was, how?

"No luck inside," Eric shouted from the other end of the corridor. "I'm going to leave several of my people searching inside the lodge in case she came back, but the rest of us are headed out. And Neil's here with his group. They're starting at the bottom of the foothills and working their way up. We're going to the top and start working our way down."

"I'll start on the middle ground, see if I can track anything," Mark said. "Angela's with me." In front of everyone he gave her a tender kiss on the lips, wishing it was the time and place for more, then dashed off to huddle with Neil and Eric for another moment, as the three of them took one final look at the grid they'd laid out for the search.

"He doesn't scowl anymore," Emoline said. "I wondered why. Guess I have my answer now."

Emoline had her answer. So did Angela. But her answer came with so many other questions...questions she didn't have time to think about right now.

"Time to take a break," Mark said, dropping down into a bed of pine needles. They'd been searching for three hours, nonstop. The area was relatively small, because Mark, Eric and Neil all agreed that Aimee wouldn't have wandered very far. She was too young, would have been too frightened and too cold. So the search assignments were specific and the areas fairly limited. But with so many places to hide...behind rocks, under bushes...the search was exhaustive, and everyone was literally turning over everything they encountered on their various paths. It was slow. Frustrating. Somber.

"Do you suppose Karen is lying about this?" Angela

asked, dropping down next to him. "I know we considered that earlier, and maybe…"

That thought had crossed his mind. More than once. "The thing with a search is that sometimes you don't know. The best-case scenario would be that Aimee is safe and sound somewhere her mother has hidden her. But you can't count on that. I mean, what if she really is lost? Or what if Karen has hidden her somewhere that could be harmful? In a situation like this, there are always so many things to consider, and the only thing a rescuer can do is assume there's a reason to search, and hope that, ultimately, there isn't."

"Thank you for letting me come with you. I feel like I might be slowing you up, though. And if I am…"

"It's a basic search. Right now we're just walking and looking for signs. Anybody with a good eye can do it. And you're not slowing me up."

"But what you're going to teach…"

"Advanced field technique. Field medicine. Survival. It goes well beyond the looking stage. It's what I…" He stopped, swallowed hard. "I grew up searching. In some ways, it's all I've ever done."

"For whom, Mark?"

"Remember how I didn't want you to quit on Scotty?"

Angela nodded. "You were right about that. And he's doing so much better right now."

"Well, I wasn't right for the reason you think. When I was Scotty's age, my father quit on me. Simply got up one day and left. Never came back. And the thing about it was he blamed me. It wasn't a case of the child taking on the blame for his parents' separation. My old man came right out and told me it was my fault he was leaving, that he'd had enough of me, that I'd taken up too much of his time. So I'm this seven-year-old kid who has absolute knowledge that it was my fault…like Scotty would have if we'd have him leave camp.

And I know you weren't going to quit on him, Angela, but that's how he would have seen it."

She shut her eyes. Shook her head. "I know. And I'm glad you argued me out of it. I wasn't…wasn't thinking."

"Don't be hard on yourself, because you were thinking… about everybody involved. It's just that I was that seven-year-old little boy who got rejected, and I know what can happen. My dad, in so many words, told me I was the worst kid in the world and I believed him, spent years trying to prove him right. I became a problem child. Not bad, but hard to handle. My mother's idea of parenting was not getting involved, so after he left I started turning myself into the child he told me I was. His rejection of me gave me free rein to be the child he rejected. But the thing was, I spent my whole childhood looking for him. When I was young, I wanted to beg him to come back, wanted to promise him I'd be a good boy. Then later on, as I got more and more angry, I wanted to confront him show him just how bad I was. I was planning it in my mind. Always searching…crowds, stores, on the street. That's all I did."

"That had to be awful," Angela said. "Did you ever find him, or did he ever come back?"

"No. By the time I was eleven or twelve, I'd given up on that and was concentrating on being that bad child he'd predicted, fully inundated in the things bad children do."

"Not bad child," she said. "Hurt child. Heartbroken child."

"Except at that age you don't understand the emotions. It was just boiling out of me in anger.

"I was shoplifting, committing vandalism, bullying… nothing serious, but things that put me well on the way to bigger crimes. And I knew I was justified because I was bad enough to break up my parents' marriage, which made stealing the occasional candy bar seem petty by comparison.

Then one day there were three of us in the corner mini-mart. One of the guys was stealing cigarettes, one was after beer. I was going for the usual candy. We were fourteen, by the way. The only thing I can say in my defense was that I didn't smoke or drink. Anyway, we were busy helping ourselves, and we got caught. It was my first time, my buddies were pros. Had been arrested a few times already. No big deal to them, but it was to me when I was taken, in handcuffs, into the courtroom to be arraigned after a night in jail, huddled in the corner with my back to the wall.

"At that point, the bad kid wasn't quite as cocky as he thought he was, and he…I was scared to death. But on my way to the courtroom, I encountered a man. To me, he just seemed strange, standing there staring at me, while I was waiting my turn to go into the court. He asked me if my parents were there to stand with me. I smarted off some stupid answer to him, and he simply smiled at me. Then he asked me if this was my first time. Naturally, I was ready to square off with him…my big, bad attitude on the defense. I told him it was my first time *getting caught*. Then he asked me the oddest question… *Will you get caught next time?*

"Next time? Did I want a next time? I'd spent the longest, roughest night of my life in the corner of that jail, and hated it. Well, I'm not sure what he saw in me, what he read in my face…he never told me. But he asked me if I wanted another chance. I didn't hesitate to say yes. And that's the day my real life started. Tom Evigan went to the judge and arranged to mentor me, while my buddies went off to lockup for six months. It seemed Tom volunteered medical services to the juvenile detention facility, which was my big break because he was the one who kept me out of jail. I can't even imagine what would have happened to me if he hadn't found me… Anyway, Tom required me to do one year cleaning his office floors, swabbing the messes, emptying trash cans. And one day a week he took me to the hospital where I…" Mark paused. Smiled, remembering. "Let's just say that my duty there was a real eye-opener for a cocky teenager. If there was a bedpan that needed to be collected, or a vomit basin rinsed out, I got the call. A whole year of that. A whole year of seeing other things going on that were…worthwhile. Tom was also the one who persuaded me to turn my searching into something useful. He was the base-camp medic for an outfit that did rescue in the California wilds, and he started letting me tag along… Saved my life literally by taking the time to help me."

Angela didn't say anything for a moment, but tears were welling in her eyes when she thought of Mark as a child who'd always looked for his father, a child who'd shouldered so much brutal blame. "I'm so sorry for all the things you went through, Mark. There's no excuse for any parent to do that to a child and I don't even know what to say except I'm glad Tom found you." She worried about Sarah, though. Would she always search for *her* father?

As if reading her thoughts, Mark reached out and squeezed her hand. "My mother was weak. Emotionally absent. But Sarah has you and you'll never let anything like what happened to me happen to her. It takes the kind of love you have for your daughter, and it doesn't matter if it's from one parent, two or an entire army. It's only about the love."

"Parenting scares me, though." Angela leaned her head against his shoulder. Liked the feel of his strength. Liked the feel of the arm that closed in around her and pulled her closer. "I keep wondering what will happen if she grows up and makes the same bad choices I did."

"We all make bad choices, but we make good ones, too. Somewhere along the way we just have to realize that the good ones outweigh the bad ones. And the good choices are never so far away when we have someone who loves us waiting, with open arms, for us to come back."

"Did you ever get over it? Over your father rejecting you?"

"Yes and no. Remember when you accused me of having those unrealistic expectations of myself? You were right. I've always put myself up there higher than anybody else, probably trying to prove to my father that I wasn't that bad kid he'd walked out on. Tom Evigan turned me around in so many ways, but he couldn't remove that hurt little boy from me. Not completely. But I don't think your ex-husband would hurt Sarah that way. You said he's not mean."

"He's not. He just doesn't want her."

"Which is something you'll have to deal with when she's old enough. Because it will have its impact, and I'm not going to lie to you about it. At some point Sarah will be hurt, but you'll be prepared to deal with it, to help her through it. And she'll know your love, Angela. That's what's important. She'll know your love."

"You knew Tom Evigan's love, and look what you've done with your life because of it. You shouldn't have had to prove yourself to anyone, not even your father." She laid her hand on his chest, over his heart. "Everything you do comes from here. And leaving medicine to shake yourself of your dad's shadow won't shake anything."

"My dad's shadow?"

"He said you were a bad boy, and after your father-in-law died and you blamed yourself, didn't that just prove it again?"

"When I leave medicine, I won't have to deal with that shadow anymore, will I?"

"But don't you love being a doctor? At the beginning of the day, and even at the end of the day, isn't that what your life is about? The thing that matters most to you?"

"What matters most is…" He shrugged. "Hell, I don't even know where I'm going, so until I do, I don't have a right to anything that matters most."

"When Brad left me, I was a mess. I wanted him back. Took him back a couple of times, only to find out that the more I was away from him, the more I didn't need him. The adversity is what made me stronger. What gave me direction. Maybe more direction than I need because I do tend to hide behind it, as I'm only beginning to realize. Nevertheless, I did have direction. Knowing what I *don't* want to be is what's turning me into what I *do* want to be. And that's what you need for yourself, Mark. Not so much a clear understanding of where you're going as a clear understanding of where you're *not* going."

"Like I said before, I didn't expect to meet you here, Angela. Didn't expect to find anything good."

She snuggled in a little closer. "The way you say it sounds like you almost think that meeting me was a bad thing."

"Not a bad thing. Maybe more of a challenge than I'd wanted at this point in my life. But *definitely* not bad." He held on tightly for a moment, then finally pushed himself up, extended a hand to Angela and pulled her along with him. "Ten minutes are up, and now it's time to get going again. And for what it's worth, I appreciate what you said. I'm not where I need to be yet, to take it to heart. But I want to, Angela. I want to because I respect you. Respect everything about you, even though I haven't been good about showing that."

"Or saying it?" she asked, smiling.

He chuckled. "You really do want a pound of my flesh, don't you?"

"More than a pound, Mark. I want much more." She brushed the pine needles off her backside. "So, lead on. I'm right behind you."

"Yeah, like I believe that one. You've been a step ahead of me from the first time I laid eyes on you. Thing is, I never realized that until now."

"But do you respect that, too?" Laughing, she grabbed up her little backpack of supplies and slung it over her shoulder.

He grabbed her by the backpack, pulled her over to him, but long enough only for a quick kiss. "I love it, and you, and my plan is to show you just how much later on. But right now I'm going to climb up there on that ridge…" he pointed to a narrow, rocky shelf above their heads "…and see if that vantage point is better than what we're seeing from down here. You go parallel to me down here."

She watched him scale the rock face. It was an easy thing for him to do. Not steep, not particularly dangerous. No harness, no equipment whatsoever. Just one man with so much ability… A lump formed in her throat as she watched him. Could she leave White Elk? Take Sarah and go with him, follow the man until the man found his dream?

If home was where the heart was, then her answer was yes. Because her heart was with Mark. And she couldn't imagine her life without him, no matter where that life took her. As much as she loved White Elk, she loved Mark Anderson more. And that was her answer, the only answer she needed.

"Head north," he shouted down to her, as he skimmed his way along the rock ledge.

She did, taking in everything around her. The pine-tree cover had let little snow in, so the walk was mostly on a bed of needles, with only snowy patches here and there. No tracks to find. No sign that anyone had come this way. But it was an easy walk, one a child might have taken. And not so far from the lodge that she couldn't run straight back there in ten minutes, if she had to. A good place to bring her camp kids...*her kids.* Another lump formed in her throat when she thought about how she might not be here in another eighteen months. She did love her JD camp, more and more every day. Even with the frustrations, like Scotty's proclivity to find food. Just last night Walt Graham had reported impressive gains in blood-sugar control for all but a couple of the children. Physical activity was up, eating problems were stabilizing. All in all, her kids were getting healthier and she couldn't wait for the six-week interval, when they'd all have a follow-up A1C test. She was expecting big things. Good things.

But she was expecting good things with Mark, too. Things that would be good for the rest of her life. And even though he hadn't asked her to come with him, she knew he would. For her, for Sarah, going with him would be a good decision. The right decision.

They'd gone several hundred feet when she spotted something in the rock. Not an opening so much as a crack. "Mark," she called up to him, "I see something. Down here...not sure..." She dashed off the trail, went straight to the rock face beneath him, looked at just the tiniest crevice going straight into the rock. Immediately, she flashed her light inside, didn't see anything. But the little mound of snow off to the side... was that a partial footprint in it? She couldn't tell, it was so chopped up. "Aimee," she called, not so loudly as to frighten the girl, if it turned out she'd crawled in there. "Can you hear me, sweetheart? Aimee?"

She listened. No noise.

Mark came down off the ledge in an instant, and knelt beside her. "Anything?" he whispered.

Angela shook her head, but pointed to the area where the snow was disturbed.

He arched his eyebrows in admiration. "Aimee, it's

Dr. Mark. We've come to take you home now. Can you hear me?"

They listened. Still, nothing.

"Aimee?" he tried again. "If you're in there, please tell me so we can come get you."

This time there was a faint rustling. "An animal?" Angela asked, looking at the size of the opening. "Nothing much larger than a small animal could have crawled in there, could it?"

He shook his head. "Aimee?"

This time the response was a tiny moan, and his heart pumped an extra beat. The problem was, he was too large to fit the opening. And even if he could get through, if the passage narrowed in there, he might end up being the one who needed rescuing. "Eric," he said, into his walkie-talkie, "I'm pretty sure we've got her located, don't know her condition, haven't seen her yet, but we've also got a problem. She's crawled into a crevice, and I don't think she's coming out of there on her own. I can't get in, and we need someone small enough—"

"I'm small enough," Angela said without hesitation.

Mark shook his head, and continued talking to Eric. "I'm not sure who you've got, but we're talking tiny."

"I'm tiny," Angela interrupted.

"But not experienced. Look, Angela…"

"Neil's got a couple of people with him who might work," Eric said. "Let me get that taken care of and I'll get back to you."

"So we just sit here and wait?" Angela snapped. "You're too big, so we just have to sit here twiddling our thumbs? Because I can do this, Mark. I can go in, see what kind of shape she's in, maybe comfort her…"

"I said no!"

"I'm not your father, Mark. I'm not going in and never

coming back. There's a child in there who needs me. Needs you to let me do this. She could be injured. Broken bones. Hypothermic. Concussion. I've studied those things, I know what they're about, and I know what they can do to a child her age. She's been out for hours, maybe suffering exposure, and for your information I know about that, too. And I can do this because I have you here to help me." She took a deep breath. "So let me go. More than that, Mark. Help me go."

Mark studied her for a moment. The hardness in his eyes softened and he shook his head in surrender then smiled. "You do have me, Angela. Now, put on your climbing harness," he said. "Just like I taught you. You'll wear it in and if you can't get out on your own, I'll pull you out."

She pulled the harness from the pack she'd brought along, strapped the belts on, did all the double-backs without a struggle, even though her hands were shaking. This time it was for real. It made a difference. She had to get it right because, trained or not, she *was* a mountain rescuer. She had a life to save.

As she got ready, Mark was on the radio to Neil, giving him their location. And his last words were, "I'm sending Angela in. She's the one we're going to rely on to get Aimee out of there." He clicked off, turned to Angela and, without a thought, tested her belts. "You ready?"

She nodded. Smiled. "The question is, are you?"

His answer was a kiss to her cheek. "I really didn't want to fall in love with you, Angela Blanchard. You know that, don't you?"

She laughed. "And I really didn't want to fall in love with you, either." In that instant before she dropped to her knees to start crawling, when their eyes met, everything that needed to be said between them was said. The longings recognized, the needs acknowledged. The love fully realized. Words weren't imperative because one brief look told the story. To break the moment, to return to her concentration, which she desperately needed now, Angela pointed down to the knee pads she'd thought to include. "See, I'm not as ill prepared as you thought I was."

"I've thought a lot of things about you, but ill prepared was never one of them." He watched her crawl into the narrow opening. "Just remember, if it's dangerous, if you don't think you can do something, don't. The cardinal rule of any rescue is to never, ever put yourself in a position that you're the one who needs rescuing."

Words she took seriously as she crawled in, down on all fours, pushing her flashlight out front of her then crawling up to meet it. Repeating the same steps, over and over. She'd hoped that once she got in, the opening might get wider, but she was disappointed to find that the widening was only a few inches. She was, essentially, crawling into a cold, dark, damp chamber that brushed along both her shoulders, and only allowed her to rise high enough to be on her knees.

Why would a child, especially a shy child like Aimee Landry, have come into a place like this? The only answer that came to mind made her angry. She was trying to escape, and this seemed safer than where she had been...which was with her mother. "Aimee," she called, "can you hear me? My name is Angela, and I'm coming in to get you. Are you hurt?"

The answer didn't come as Angela had hoped. In fact, the only noise in the tunnel was what she was making...her breathing, the way her shoulders brushed the rock walls on either side of her, the clanking of the metal on her harness. Her own grunts of effort. The flashlight scraping over the rock floor. The noises amplified. Got louder. Nearly thundered in her ears. Yet when she stopped, everything became so deathly quiet that chills leapt up her arms, down her back, through her legs. "Aimee," she whispered, then paused while her voice bounced ahead of her, echoing on the rocks, getting softer and softer until it died out. "Can you hear me?"

She shut her eyes, held her breath to listen, and the nothingness amplified in the pitch dark. It was all around her, so still. And that stillness was so deafening. "Aimee?"

She listened again. Held her breath again. Felt the blackness closing in on her again, but this time… Was that a moan? Had Aimee moaned, or was that her imagination playing tricks on her? "I'm coming, sweetheart," she said, doubling the speed of her crawling. As if the Three Sisters had reached down into the very center of their core to help her, the chamber seemed to open a little. Her shoulders no longer touched the sides of the passageway, her back no longer scraped the roof. To her ears, her breathing gained volume. She could hear her heart beating, and feel it pounding in her temples. She was so close. So very close… "Aimee…"

"Help," the little voice whispered from the darkness.

But where? She trained the light straight ahead, saw nothing. Looked left and right, hoping to find a hollow of some sort, but was greeted with flat rock everywhere. "Where are you?"

No answer.

"Aimee, where are you? You have to tell me."

"She'll be mad."

She was so close to the voice she could almost reach out and touch it. "She's not going to be mad at you, Aimee."

"But I didn't do what she said."

Angela gave her flashlight another shove ahead, and it fell down…down into some kind of hole. Immediately, she grabbed a tiny penlight from her pocket, Mark's penlight. And shined it down. There, just five feet below her, Aimee Landry lay huddled in a fetal position, clasping a teddy bear. Shivering so hard Angela could see it from her vantage point.

"Found her!" she shouted back to Mark. He wasn't so far away, really. Maybe fifty feet. Fifty feet that seemed like forever. "She's in a hole. I'm going to climb down."

"Is she injured?" he yelled back.

"Can't tell. I'll let you know in a minute."

"How deep?"

"Just a few feet. I'll be fine."

"No chances, Angela. Don't take any chances."

Chances? Climbing down into the hole to get Aimee wasn't taking a chance. But spending the rest of her life with Mark was, and she was ready to do that. Ready to take the biggest chance of her life. "I'm going down."

The climb was easy. More like a slide down the rock to the bottom. And once there the first thing she did was find her flashlight, rattle it, get it to flash back on. Then she went to Aimee, didn't scoop her up as she wanted to. Instead, she went about a very methodical examination. "Are you hurt?"

"Yes," the girl whimpered.

"Can you tell me where."

"My leg hurts. And my arm and head. And I'm cold."

Angela immediately pulled off her outer layer, a quilted vest, and laid it over Aimee. Then she grabbed her personal little first-aid kit out of her pack, pulled out the thermometer, and took Aimee's temperature. "Her temperature's ninety-six," she called out.

"You have a thermometer?" he called back, sounding quite amazed.

"I brought my first-aid kit. And her pulse is one-twenty. Respirations forty. All a little high, but I've covered her up so that may help. Can she have water, Mark?"

"No, not yet. We need to check her for internal injuries."

Angela looked at Aimee's legs, didn't see anything

remarkable except cuts and bruises. But her arm... There was a slight crook in the forearm. Aimee flinched when Angela ran gentle fingers over it. "Is that where it hurts the worst?"

Aimee nodded.

"Well, I have something that might just make it feel a little better." She knew it wouldn't, but she'd read about the placebo effect, telling a patient something they wanted to hear in the hope they believed it, even though what was being told might necessarily be a little white lie. "This scarf around my neck...it's magical. That's why I wear it, because it always makes me feel better." She pulled the knit scarf off, tied it gently and loosely around Aimee's arm, more a buffer from any bumps she might sustain while they took her out of there. "If it makes your arm feel better, you can keep it on for as long as you like."

Aimee didn't say anything, but Angela could see the scarf working its 'miracle' as Aimee's sniffles lessened a little. "Now, does your tummy hurt?" she asked.

"No. But I'm hungry."

"Well, that's something we'll be able to take care of once we get you to the hospital. You tell me what your favorite thing to eat is, and if Dr. Mark says it's OK, I'll make it for you myself."

"I like peanut-butter sandwiches. With jelly. Grape jelly. And chocolate brownies."

"Those just happen to be the best things I make. But like I said, we'll have to ask Dr. Mark first."

"OK."

"Her belly feels normal," she called to Mark. "Nothing rigid. She says it doesn't hurt, but she does have a broken arm."

"With a magic scarf," Aimee reminded her.

"A broken arm with a magic scarf on it," Angela called.

"And we'd like peanut-butter and grape-jelly sandwiches and chocolate brownies as soon as we can manage that!"

"She's amazing," Eric said, as a group of about twenty people gathered around, ready to do whatever was necessary to get Angela and Aimee out of the cave. "Are you sure you don't want her in your class? Because I think…"

Mark shot Eric a look of total surrender. "You knew all along, didn't you?"

"I married her sister. Didn't stand a chance after I met her. Figured since heredity usually wins out, you might get as lucky as I did. So, is this where I welcome you to the family?"

"Do I need to call Gabrielle and tell her to start making wedding plans, that her best friend is getting married?" Neil asked.

"Maybe I should propose first," Mark suggested. "Preferably *after* we get everybody out of the cave."

"You warmed up yet?" Mark asked, pulling the blanket up over Angela's shoulders.

She was tucked into her bed at the lodge, with Fred curled up next to her, feeling more lazy than anything else. Today, Dr. James Galbraith was taking over her JD camp, assisted by more people than she could count. Doctor's orders, she was to spend the day in bed, resting. But she didn't mind it very much. Especially as Mark hadn't left her side since the previous evening. Twelve hours, and he'd been waiting on her hand and foot, probably watching her sleep, taking care of Sarah. Everything nice.

"I'm perfect. Haven't stayed in bed this long since I can't remember when."

"Someone needs to take care of you."

"Someone needs to quit worrying about me. I'm fine. How's Aimee?"

"Except for the fact that they can't get that magic scarf off her, she's great. The fracture isn't serious, she's warmed up nicely, they've rehydrated her, and they're going to keep her for a couple of days just to make sure everything stays good."

"And her mother?"

"In custody. They've taken her to a facility in Salt Lake City for a psychiatric evaluation. Aimee's father's here, though. He's been worried out of his mind, not knowing where Karen and Aimee were. Apparently, Karen only had visitation rights, and a couple of months ago she and Aimee simply disappeared. He hasn't left his daughter's side since he got here."

"I'm glad she has someone to take care of her. You're sure he's…?"

"He's a good man. And a very grateful man that his daughter was rescued."

Mark sat down on the side of the bed, nudged Fred to the foot, and handed Sarah over to Angela. It felt so good to hold her daughter. But it also felt good knowing that in all these hours when she'd been sleeping, Mark had been the one holding Sarah. Sarah loved him and there was no mistaking the emotion she saw in him for Sarah. "I had the oddest phone call from Gabby a little while ago," she said, scooting over to make room for Mark to lie down next to her.

"About?"

"Wedding plans."

"Oh, that."

"That? My best friend is making wedding plans for me and, as far as I know, I'm not getting married."

"Well, Dinah's doing the same thing, and I've heard that the twins are all excited about being flower girls. They're pretty sure Sarah's going to be included in the wedding party, too, and they're making plans for teaching her how to throw rose petals."

Angela glanced at Sarah, who was busy pestering Fred. "Do you know anything about this wedding, young lady?"

Sarah totally ignored her, so she looked at Mark. "Am I the last one here to know something I should have probably been the first one to know?"

He stretched out beside her, put his arm around her and pulled her into his side. "Well, Neil, Eric and I talked it over when you were in the cave, and—"

"And just assumed?"

"What did you want me to do? Shout out something like, *Angela, will you marry me?* I mean, I thought that should be saved for a more private moment."

"Gabby said Emoline is already working on flower arrangements, and Helen Baxter has pledged the grand ballroom as the first event when it opens up again."

"OK, so maybe we should have talked about this before I mentioned anything to my friends, but you're the one who knows White Elk better than I do. You know how people get involved. So it's not my fault."

"Say it again."

"What?"

"The part where you're shouting into the cave."

"You mean, *Angela, will you marry me?*"

She nodded. "It has a nice sound to it, doesn't it? Makes me feel…included. So tell me, has anybody set a date for us, or do we have to do that for ourselves?"

"Not a date so much as a house. We have a house. Let's see…how did that happen? Eric's sister got married recently, she and her husband bought a new house together, and we're going to get Eric's brother-in-law's old house? It's large, rambling, perfect for lots of kids. Something like that, anyway."

She rolled over, propped herself up on an elbow to look at him. "You've made an offer on a house? But I thought…"

"That I'd still want to leave, and take you and Sarah with me? Remember when I said I'd just keep going until I found it, but I didn't know what it was going to be? Let's just say that while *it* wasn't love at first sight, *it* snuck up on me anyway."

"And you're happy? Because I've been doing a lot of thinking, and if you still need to travel, I can do that. We can do that."

"But there's nothing out there to look for. I found it here, and I like being here."

"I know Brad will let you adopt Sarah, if that's what you want to do."

"He's an idiot," Mark said, kissing Angela on the forehead. "Of course I want to adopt her. She's part of you and I love her. Although I'm not sure how I'm going to manage two of you. Actually, the three of you since Mr. Whetherby's going into an assisted living facility and isn't going to be able to take Fred with him. Which means Fred's now part of this family, too. Of course, I've got lots of friends in White Elk, people who can help me, if I need it. Especially if…"

"If what?"

"If we have another daughter or two just like you."

"You want girls?"

"Or boys." He fished a folded paper from his pocket and handed it to her. "But I think we're going to have to wait for a little while. Because it's going to be vigorous, and I absolutely will not allow a pregnant lady into my class."

She looked at the paper. Frowned. "What's going to be vigorous?"

"Your classes. That's your class schedule, by the way. We've decided to stay up at Juniper Lodge rather than doing the class work at the hospital, so your JD camp won't interfere with your rescue classes since it will all be happening at the same place."

"But I thought...I mean, I know I don't have the skill level you need."

"You took a thermometer with you, Angela. And a magic scarf. The one thing that I didn't want to see in you was your raw skill. But it's there. You're going to be brilliant out in the field, especially with some tutoring on the side."

She arched playful eyebrows. "Know anybody who wants to tutor me?"

He raised his hand. "But don't get any ideas. I'm soon to be a very happily married man, if the woman I've proposed to ever gets around to saying yes."

"Yes," she whispered. "To everything, yes."

"Yes, Daaa..." Sarah chimed in.

"Daaa is right," Angela said. And never, ever had a name sounded so good. "Happiness," she said. "A word of Middle English origin meaning contentment, love, satisfaction, pleasure, or joy."

"And which of those describe you?"

"All of them," she said, snuggling into Mark while Sarah and Fred played at the end of the bed. "Every last one of them."